The Companions
We Lose

A Horror Novella

Micah Castle

Content warnings are available at the end of this book.

No use of AI was used in creation of this book.

ISBN: 979 8 9924823-1-7

Written by Micah Castle

Edited by Rachel Oestreich (The Wall Flower Editing)

Cover Art by Red Lagoe

Published by Anhedonia Press

WARNING: READ FIRST

To my beautiful wife, Nikki, who without her I would be nothing.

ACKNOWLEDGMENTS

Thanks to the authors, editors, *people* I've worked or talked with or talked to over the years. You've helped this book come to fruition.

Thanks to JT, JD, and the Kids.

Thanks to my Patreon supporters, you guys keep the fire going: David S., Jocelyn C., Rosina S., Shaun R., Black Book Sculpts, Claudia C., Kylie L., Nik C., Tasha

Unfortunately, I can't list everyone, but thanks to those I've befriended in the writing world (in no particular order): Gwendolyn Kiste, Scott J. Moses, Kyle Winkler, Matt Wildasin, Elford Alley, Emma Editrix, Mindy Rose, Briana Morgan, Katherine Silva, Michael Wehunt, David Peak, Alex Woodroe, Matt Blairstone, Alan Lastufka, Joe Koch, Zach Graham, Matt Vaughn, and so many others.

CHAPTER 1

Michael hesitates before turning on the kitchen lights. He doesn't want to see Zylo, his beloved dog, but must look to help him. *Click.* Under the fluorescents, it's worse than he could've imagined. Zylo's underbelly is split from groin to neck, two wilted flaps of flesh, fat, and muscle. Coagulated blood pooled beneath him. Someone *cut* him open. It wasn't a hit-and-run, an accident; some bastard held him down and used a knife—Michael forces himself to not look away, to bear witness to the horror his good boy has become. Within the gaping maw was... Nothing—no sign of innards whatsoever, gloom hiding the inner walls. Not only did that fucker *disembowel* him, but *stole* them, too.

"What the *fuck*!" He collapses to his knees. "Who the fuck steals organs?" He lurches to the wall, grabs the phone from its cradle, and dials 9-1-1.

"Hello, you've reached the—"

"Someone killed my dog!" He presses the phone against his face. "Somebody..." Sobs overwhelm him.

"Sir, where are you located?..."

"Sir, are you there?"

"1723," he croaks. "1723 Tulip Avenue. Carlysle City."

"We'll send some—"

He lets the phone dangle on its spiral cord, smacking the wall. As much as he wants to see Zylo, because who knows how much longer he has the chance to, he can't keep the lights on any longer. Michael hits the switch, submerging the room in darkness. Illuminance still dimly falls through the small window above the sink, but shadows hide what's come to pass.

Too beat to go anywhere else, Michael lies on the floor in the fetal position. He closes his eyes, moaning, cursing, letting tears run down his face...

Cold pavement digs into his knees, blood soaking into his striped pajamas. The streetlights cast their wide shadows across the sleeping road. Curtains remain closed. Porch lights off. No siren in the distance, no red-and-blue lights coming up the street.

The boy scrapes his knuckles on the gravel putting his hands beneath his limp pup. Wide, glassy pale blue eyes looking up at the boy but not seeing him. His mouth hangs open, the tongue the boy loved to get kisses from dangles. The boy rocks back and forth, holding his companion tightly against his chest, getting more blood on his pajamas.

He lifts his loved one in his arms when he stands, and carries him toward the open front door, all the while whispering into the night, unto deaf ears, about love, grief, guilt, but more importantly, anger, hurt— retribution.

Hammering on the door wakes Michael. "Police department," a man calls. "We got a call."

He inhales sharply, as though he hadn't breathed while he was asleep. How the hell did he fall asleep to begin with? His body groans when he stands. He wipes his face on his sleeve, plodding to and opening the door.

"Evening," the heavyset police officer says. He wears black pants, a golden badge clipped to the belt, and a soft blue shirt under a dark jacket. "I'm Officer Wollah with the Carlysle City PD, we got a call—"

"About Zylo, I know," he says. "Come in and look."

Each step is like wading through ankle-deep mud. The weight of the world presses more onto his shoulders the closer he gets to the table. Wollah's speaking behind him but it's lost in a veil of white noise settling over Michael's mind, dust in his ears. It's like he relives the events that happened a few hours ago, but now with the foresight of what's to come. What he will and won't find. In the kitchen, Michael swipes the switch, but looks away, focusing on the cabinets above the counter.

"This the dog?"

Of course it's the fucking dog. "Yes, that's Zylo."

Michael hears Wollah grunt as he must crouch in front of the table. "Sweet Jesus..." the officer mutters. "What happened to it?"

"What it looks like. Someone cut him open."

"There's nothing inside." Grunting again, he straightens. "So what would you like us to do? Call animal control and have them come get it, or give you the number for the vet so you can call them and get it cremated?"

His temples throb as he faces Wollah. "I want you to find out who did this."

He sighs. "You don't want to do that for just a dog."

Just a dog? Just a damn dog?

He clenches his fists, keeps his hands from shaking. "He wasn't *just* a dog. Zylo was more than that."

"Look," he says, "I get it, but lemme be straight with you. What happened to it is awful, and even if we found the guy who did this, he'd only be looking at a hefty fine or a couple years of jail time—if you're lucky, both."

A fine? A fucking fine!

"But without photos, videos, any sort of evidence, it'll be near impossible to find the sicko who killed your mutt."

"Then what *can* I do?"

He scratches his bristled cheek. "You could still make a report, I suppose."

"Then let's do that."

Michael hears the beginning of a groan, but it remains in Wollah's throat. He removes a pad and pen from his back pocket, flips to a blank page. "First, what's your first and last name?"

"Michael Green."

"Your occupation?"

"Unemployed, but I used to be a writer."

He scribbles, then: "Now we got that outta the way, from the get-go, tell me what happened to the dog—"

"*Zylo.*"

He waves his hand in front of his face. "Yeah, got it."

Michael recounts the events: letting Zylo out, falling asleep on the couch for no more than an hour, then coming outside to find him on the road, disemboweled.

"Were you drinking or on any drugs?"

He shakes his head.

"Anyone you know who may want to hurt you or your dog?"

"No, no one I know would do such a fucked-up thing."

"Well... Okay," he says, shoving his notes and pen into his front pocket. "That's all I need. I'll file a report at the station, and we'll go from there."

Something comes to mind. "Wait, aren't you going to take a hair sample or something?"

Wollah glances toward the table. "We only do that for *human* victims, plus our lab isn't equipped for that."

"Then, I'd like an autopsy done."

"You don't need one. I can tell you right now what killed it."

You dense mother— "I know that, but I want to know *everything*. Time of death, how exactly it happened, if there's any fibers that shouldn't be there, and so on."

"You'd call the vet for that, I think."

"Great," he says. "I'll do that, *thanks*."

"Not a problem," Wollah says, "I'll get working on that report." He begins leaving. "Good luck with the vet, and merry Christmas."

Michael doesn't bother to try to stop him, because what would be the point? He watches from the entry as the officer crosses the walkway outside, avoiding the puddle of Zylo's blood on the street to get into his car.

"Useless." Michael slams the door.

Although Michael doesn't want to hide him, he uses an old bedsheet to cover Zylo. After crying once more, he calls Pet General. He doesn't realize it's four in the morning until he receives the automated message: *"Hello, I'm sorry but we're currently closed. You can call again..."* Cursing himself for being stupid, he hangs up.

He turns off the kitchen lights and avoids the room at all costs. Instead, he paces the living room, the hallway, and the upstairs. He wishes for sleep but the bed's also somewhere he doesn't want to be. Another place where his misery will fester and grow. First it was his ex-wife, Kayla, and his son, Aaron, who left him, and now it was Zylo. An ever-expanding void that shouldn't exist but does because of his own actions.

Zylo wasn't my fault.

"It was, it is."

I couldn't have done anything.

"I could've been awake."

I fell asleep by accident.

"Been paying attention."

It. Was. An. Accident.

"I could've fucking let him out the back or told him no and let him piss and shit on the floor! I'd clean a thousand messes rather than him being gone!"

He halts in front of the open bedroom door. Zylo's lion squeaky toy lies by Michael's dresser, his water and half-eaten food dish by the far wall, his bed in front of the heat vent. The blankets on Michael's bed are in a nest, where his pup loved to sleep when he left the house.

Michael closes the door.

Passing the office he hasn't used in a while, he goes into the bathroom, switching on the lights. He doesn't want to look at himself, but he feels like he must; like he must burn into his memory what he looks like tonight, the day of Zylo's passing, as some sort of punishment for being negligent.

Dry blood smears his pale, stubbled face; deep-seated, bleary brown eyes with dark bags underneath; greasy brown hair, unwashed in what feels like days; his lower lip crusted with blood. Looking at his pink-tinged hands, it's as though he stares at someone else's extremities, the waxy flesh wrapped around a stranger's knobby fingers.

Finally he turns on the tap, and with scalding water he scrubs his face and hands in the sink until they're red. Then he undresses, leaving the bloody clothes on the floor, and puts on a black thermal under a sweater, sweatpants, and thick socks from the hamper, not caring if they're dirty. Michael has always run cold, but in December, it wasn't *only* cold for him, but freezing.

At the upstairs window on the landing, he idles. Outside, the street-lamp illuminates the scarlet stain on the pavement. He clenches his jaw. His skin prickles. Soon, he has a headache and thoughts rush through his mind too quickly to grasp.

Waiting...

Waiting...

What am I supposed to do? I can't leave. Could call Kayla, but I shouldn't this late. I can take some of my anxiety meds, but God only knows the hell that'll bring if I take too much. I can't deal with being sleepy... Not now.

"I have to find who killed Zylo."

Michael wants to scream but stay silent, wants to disappear into the night and never come back but remain inert, wants to do nothing but also figure everything out. Why is he desperate for opposites simultaneously? Why is his mind bombarding him with indiscernible longings he shouldn't succumb to? Why put ideas in his head that're irrational?

Why?

Why?

Why?

"She'll be mad, but fuck it."

He trudges downstairs, grabs the kitchen phone, pulls it into the hallway, and calls the number he still remembers after all these years.

"Michael?" Kayla's voice, groggy with sleep. He can picture her with eyes closed as she talks. "Why are you calling me at four in the morning?"

"Zylo died."

"Oh my God." More awake. *"How?"*

"Can I come over? I don't want to talk about it over the phone. I promise I won't wake Aaron."

"Yeah, of course, we can talk outside."

"Thank you," he says, and hangs up, then says to the form beneath the bed sheet: "I'll be back soon, buddy."

. . .

Kayla kept the car in the divorce, too. Aaron was only five years old, and she needed it to get to work and him to preschool. It made the most sense, but Michael couldn't afford another vehicle, so he bought a bike soon after moving out. It worked, getting him from point A to point B in a timely manner.

In spite of the late autumn cold biting into his open skin, but thankful that the snow has held off so far. The white lights strung on the gabled houses, the illuminated snowmen and Santa Clauses in the yards guiding him to thei—*her* home.

She sits out on the front porch with a comforter wrapped around her, holding a steaming cup of what smells like coffee. He gets off the bike at the walkway and sets it against the stair handrail. In the growing twilight, he notices she's exhausted, her brown eyes almost matching his. He stands at the bottom of the steps, awkwardly making eye contact. Even though it's been years since they've been together, he's tempted to go up and sit next to her and join her under the blanket.

"So tell me what happened, Michael."

As he repeats himself for the second time, he paces, stopping before the wet lawn, turning, and beginning the cycle again. He can't help but scratch his forehead, run his fingers over the sides of his mouth, pick at his cracked lips. Though he's finally doing *something*, his mind's restless, and giving in to his ticks helps a little. Kayla doesn't bother telling him to stop, knowing he won't.

Michael finishes and wipes his eyes.

"An autopsy?" she asks. "Do you think that's the best thing to do?"

"What the hell do you mean?" he spits, then makes himself calm down. *If I bite her head off, she'll leave and I'll be alone again.*

She sips from her drink. "I know you, Michael. I understand you want to know everything that there is to know, but, like... Will it help?"

"Of course it will. I'll know what happened to him, exactly. It'll help me catch who did it."

"Catch them? Shouldn't you let the cops deal with that?"

"The cops aren't going to do shit, Kay. They don't see him the same way I do."

She sighs. "Michael... Let's say you get the autopsy done, then what? What're you going to do with that information?"

Michael glances at the ground. *What will I do...?*

"I haven't thought that far, but I will, when it happens. Plus, what'll it hurt, anyway? It might put my mind at ease."

"Maybe, Michael, or maybe it'll make things worse, too. I'd hate to see that happen to you after this."

"I don't think it will," he quickly says, running his shoe over the damp grass bordering the sidewalk.

"What if the autopsy doesn't give you the answer you want? Will you be able to let it go?"

Not until I find them. "Yeah."

"You sure? Before therapy, you—"

"*I'm positive, Kay.* It won't be like then, I'm better now."

"And you have the money to do this?"

No, but I have a credit card. "I have enough, but if you want to chip in, you can."

"*You can't be*—" Kayla pauses, then: "I know you loved him and he meant a lot to you. I loved him, too, but what I get from the store goes straight to buying Aaron the things *he* needs."

"You know I'll give you more when—"

She waves her hand. "It's fine. I'm not asking you for anything, but I can't help you that way."

Silence befalls them.

Michael picks bark from the oak in her yard, and peels apart fallen leaves. Kayla finishes her coffee. Despite the talk, he still feels on edge. He knows she's right. If Zylo's autopsy doesn't answer the questions he has, it'll be an all-encompassing obsession, an impossible itch he must scratch until it's bleeding. But he refuses to admit that aloud. Last thing he needs is for Kayla to be on him about what he should or shouldn't do with his life. *She left me, so she doesn't have a say anymore.*

The sky turns periwinkle blue. Birds chirp, cars start. The world slowly awakens around them.

"I'm sorry," she finally says, raising to her feet, "but I gotta get ready for work, and get Aaron up for school in an hour."

He nods. "It's fine. Just wanted to talk to you, you know. Tell you what's going on with Zylo."

"Thanks." She stops at the front door. "Let me know if you need anything or have an update."

He aims his bike toward the street. "Thanks, Kayla."

"Oh," she says, before entering the house. "I'll make sure not to mention it to Aaron."

"Oh, yeah—don't, please. He loved him almost as much as me."

Then she's inside, the door closes, and through the front door window the entry light pops on. Michael gets back onto his bike, and returns home.

The house reeks of rot. He gags as he rushes to open the living room window. Morning chill slips in, and he turns up the heat. Since it takes a while, he keeps his coat. Michael keeps his sight away from Zylo and takes the phone into the dining room, pulling the plastic cord taut. Presses redial.

"Hello, this is Pet General. My name's Mackenzie, how can I help you?"

"Yeah, hi, Mackenzie, my name's Michael Green. Zylo, my dog, died—"

"Oh, I'm sorry to hear that."

"Thanks. I'd like an autopsy done. The police said I should call you."

"Sure, I can schedule you one, but I'll need some information from you first. What was Zylo's cause of death?"

Michael bites his bottom lip. He debates giving her specific details, how awkward it'll sound coming out of his mouth. Instead, he says: "He was murdered."

"Oh, Jesus, I'm so sorry. Are the police looking for who did it?"

"Yeah, they're already on it."

"Good, I hope they get him." Papers flitter on the other end of the phone. "Now about that appointment, can you hold for me a minute?"

Before he can say sure, crackling classical music plays. He pinches the phone between his head and shoulder, and moves into the kitchen and starts making coffee. He knows he should try to sleep instead of having caffeine, but...

"Sleeping's a waste of time," he mumbles.

"Sir? We have an opening at eleven. Does that work for you?"

The clock above the back door reads six thirty a.m. Too soon. Not enough time to prepare not only his pup but himself. He needs more time to finalize the plan. Panic swells in Michael as he strides around the kitchen table, keeping his vision glued to the floor. Sweat forms under his arms.

Should I wait until I have something more definite?

Try tomorrow, or the next day? That'd be enough time, maybe, but can I leave him like this for that long?

Or would now be better?

Get it done, then be closer to finding who did this?

Fine, yes, today. It has to be today.

"That works," he practically gasps.

"Eleven it is. I'll see you and Zylo then."

They hang up.

Shit, wait. How am I getting him there? His mind fires in all directions, attempting to configure a plan for how he'll manage to get Zylo to the vet without a car.

I can't ask Kayla, definitely not, she has work and Aaron. I don't need to burn her any more than I have to.

I haven't talked to anybody for a while, and everyone lives too far away to be asking for that kind of favor.

Could carry him, but it's like ten miles away. And freezing.

Strap him to the bike somehow? No, no, that wouldn't work.

The bus? The bus, maybe. But, how would I manage that? Wrap him in blankets and scented trash bags? That'll work, the best I can do.

The coffee finishes percolating. Michael finally stops and gazes at Zylo before beginning the process of getting him ready for travel. Rigor mortis has already set in, and ignoring his back wailing, Michael softly sets him onto another sheet he had laid on the floor.

Carefully, he wraps him in it, then Michael uses lavender-scented trash bags to cover each end of him, tying their pull strings tightly together. "If anyone was watching me right now, this'd look so damn stupid." He nearly forgets that they'll need his hair to compare to for testing, so he snips a few strands into a ziplock bag and puts it in his pocket. And, since he held the bag, they'll have his fingerprints, too. *Killing two birds with one stone.*

By nine a.m., he carried Zylo into the entry and set him by the door. He finishes the pot of coffee and a fresh one brews. He doesn't believe he can keep any food down, but force-feeds himself a bowl of oatmeal while staring aimlessly out the window above the sink. In the neighbor's yard, a small red doghouse sits alone in the patchy grass, the lead lying on the ground. Usually their white terrier is outside at this time. Michael didn't let him out the back to avoid the dog yelping at him. *Must've brought him in because of the weather.*

After rinsing out the bowl and drinking more caffeine, he closes the living room window, returns to the entry and sits on the bottom stair, putting on his shoes. "Remember your first vet appointment?" Tears line his eyes. "I remember you were so excited to go for a ride, and we thought that when we got there you'd freak out, but you were so good... Gave kisses to the vet, didn't bark at the other animals—remember that ferret?" Michael laughs. "We put him on your back and you carried him around the waiting room, and—and, after we got a pup cup from McDonalds. You loved those."

He stood, legs weak. "Guess it's time for your final visit, boy."

Luckily the bus comes soon after he arrives at the stop, and he gets on by sidestepping through the parted door while carrying his dog. The gaunt driver and the other passengers quietly watch Michael make his way to the back of the bus, placing Zylo on the row of seats, and runs back to the front to pay.

"All good?" the bus driver says.

"Yup," Michael says, and keeps his head down when he hurries back and sits by his pup.

An old woman in a side seat turns away from him, a stout man on the opposite side keeps his eyes on his newspaper, but a nearby teenager, whose headphones blare with rock music, continues to look at the mysterious form wrapped in trash bags.

Michael debates saying something, but doesn't want conflict. And who cares, really, if the girl stares? As long as Zylo doesn't smell and there are no tears in the plastic, it's fine.

He rests his hand on him, peering out the window. Weathered gabled houses and browning oak trees pass by, soon replaced by empty, debris-littered lots and abandoned businesses. The smell of sulfur tinges the air, and in the distance the smokestacks jutting from the steel mill belch smoke. Passengers jerk and slide as the bus goes over and avoids potholes, taking wide turns and stopping abruptly. Unlit green, silver, and red-tinseled decorations of Christmas trees, bells, and candy canes are attached to the street poles. A small restaurant with Thanksgiving decorations still in their windows goes past, then shuttered shopfronts and a used car dealership.

Michael almost misses his stop and quickly yanks on the overhead wire. The bus throws him forward, and hisses as it lowers. He heaves Zylo into his arms and gets out of the bus and onto the curb. He keeps to the alley running behind the stores, avoiding people and cars. After coming out onto the sidewalk, he finds the Pet General sign hanging from the corner of a redbrick building, and goes in.

"Hello," a woman says from behind the glass-top counter. Her eyes widen when Michael puts him onto the counter. "And, who is this?"

"Hi, yes, my name's Michael Green—it's Zylo. I called earlier about getting an autopsy done. You're Mackenzie, right?"

She smiles. "Yes, that's me, and I remember now. Let me get someone to bring him to the back."

"Wait," he says. "Before that, do you know what the vet will do to him?"

"I'm not sure. I just work the front desk, but I can have the vet come out and talk to you before they take him back, if you like."

"Wonderful, thank you."

She disappears down the hall. Framed photographs and illustrations hang on the walls, of various breeds of dogs galloping in flowery fields, catching frisbees in midair, staring into the camera with wide, black eyes... Michael glances over to the empty waiting room. Magazines are sprawled on the short tables in between threadbare chairs, and squeaky toys and enamel bones tucked under a few in bins, waiting for a good boy to gnaw on them.

His chest hitches. Sighs. Everything here reminds him of Zylo. They only took him to the vet for routine checkups and his shots, otherwise he was healthy, but *damn...* He wipes his eyes.

"Fuck," he says under his breath.

"Mr. Green?" Mackenzie says, now behind the counter. Two men in blue scrubs stand near her. He faces her, sniffles. "The vet said he'd go over the details of the procedure with you over the phone. He's busy with another patient, and he doesn't know when he'll be available. Does that work for you?"

He nods.

"Can we take him back now?"

But he's going to be alone back there.

Who's going to be with him, if anyone?

I don't want him to be there by himself, stored away like a box.

He's not a box. He's Zylo—my dog.

But he says: "That's fine." *It's not. This isn't okay. This can't be okay.*

"You'll have to let go, sir," one of the men says, and Michael notices he's clenching the bags.

Overwhelming grief screams for him not to, as though this moment is truly when Zylo's gone and not last night, that this is the final time he'll ever see him, *be* with him. He won't be at home when he opens the front door. He won't bark to be let outside. He won't beg for Michael's food. He won't be beside him when he sleeps or when he wakes up. He won't have zoomies and sprint around the house or the yard. His leash will hang on the hook forever. His toys will never be played with. His treats will never be enjoyed. He—

"Sir, please?"

"Sorry." He finally lets go, and he steps back to let the two take him. They walk down the hall, and vanish into a room at the end. When the door closes it's like someone broke a baseball bat over his chest.

The woman places a tablet and pen onto the counter. "Whenever you're ready, you'll need to fill out this form with your information, and how would you like your pet returned to you. He's not going away forever, okay?"

Her words don't reassure him, and he isn't sure if he nods. The pen feels wrong in his hand, like he's wearing a glove of fake flesh, but he manages to fill out the paper.

Mail.

Cremation.

"That's—" he starts, tongue numb. Something sour's stuck in the back of his throat. Michael hands her the tablet with the bag of his hair, and runs a hand down his face. "That's for any sort of testing they do, but anyway, when will the vet call?"

"Should be before three."

"And if everything goes well, how long would the autopsy take?"

"I'm not sure, but not too long. He'll be sent to you within a week or two, though."

Not the way he should be. As ashes in a little wooden box, and a clay imprint of his paw that he can hang by a string or have on the desk never uses. A remembrance of how those very paws carried him running, let him leap, to scratch at the door when Michael was unlocking it, coming home. Any amount of time was eons to his dog, as though five minutes were five years. No one ever felt that way about Michael, not even Kayla or Aaron. Zylo's devotion and love was truly endless.

Crossing the street, he takes a left at the corner and goes straight until he arrives at the old brown brick police station. Up a small flight of stairs, through glass double doors, and across the linoleum floor, Michael reaches the plastic-shielded front desk. A gangly woman wearing thick-rimmed glasses, her graying auburn hair in a bun, reads a TV guide behind it.

Michael taps on the counter. "Excuse me?"

The woman keeps the book open with a finger as she faces him. "How can I help you?"

"Hi, I was wondering if Officer Wollah was here? He came to my house last night about my dog."

"Let me check." She faces the computer and pecks on the keys, one by one. She presses enter as if striking a match. "Nope, not here. His shift ended at six."

"When will he be back?"

She stares at Michael over her glasses. "Why do you want to know that?"

"I want to find out if he has made any progress."

"It hasn't been a full day yet, it usually takes *weeks* for something to happen. Sometimes even *months.*"

Probably years, too.

He's not going to find the asshole who did this.

It was useless to call the police.

It was pointless answering his questions or even expecting him to help.

Didn't he say he couldn't do much without evidence anyway, and if so, they might only get a fine?

Stupid, fucking stupid. I can do more than he can.

"Thanks for the help," he says, and leaves.

By eleven o'clock, Michael's back on the bus. Gray clouds choke the sky. Howling winds cause trees to sway and store signs to rattle. The first real December snow's coming, he guesses. Zylo hasn't really been with him since yesterday, yet Michael feels like a piece of himself is missing. He puts his hand where Zylo's body lay hours ago. The seat's warm, but he's not oblivious enough to believe anything besides he's imagining it or someone recently sat there.

His knee won't stop bobbing and he can't stop picking at the skin around his fingernails. The back of his skull pounds like a drum. His limbs feel weighty, a fog clotting his mind, but he's jittery, anxious, *afraid.* Tears threaten to come again, but he refuses to do so in front of the people on the bus. His knotted stomach tries to churn.

This will be the first time coming back to an empty home. No Kayla, no Aaron, no Zylo. The palpable emptiness within those walls fills Michael with so much dread he considers not going home at all.

I have to.

The vet will call, and without that information he won't be able to find the piece of shit who killed him. That's everything to him now, for Zylo was all that he had left. Michael was always a routine person, a self-inflicted schedule etched into the core of his being. Wake up around a certain time, eat about every three or four hours, do chores on specific days, and so on.

It was tolerable with Kayla since it wasn't to a fault, but became less so when they were surprised one morning with a positive pregnancy test. Kayla was ecstatic, Michael was...*not*. With the way he was, a child hadn't been in his plans—how could he raise a kid with his rigid life-style, prioritize them over things that were highly important to him? They already had Zylo, and that was enough for him. Nevertheless despite his fears of fatherhood and inclination toward abortion, he couldn't bring himself to confess his feelings to Kayla. He hadn't seen her so happy since their wedding day, so Michael decided to try to be the best father he could be, better than his own, at least.

But the world felt otherwise. Soon after Aaron was born, the recession hit and his publisher quickly went under. Without an income, he couldn't afford bills, groceries, to support the ones he was supposed to take care of. Unemployment helped some, but still wasn't enough.

Michael frantically spent money they didn't have by submitting his older work to other publishing houses who hadn't moved to email, but all he got was either silence, template rejections, or return-to-senders. Switching gears, he tried submitting newer material instead, but received the same results, except for one editor who said that his stories felt *off*, like there was a disconnect between the author and the story, and by proxy, story to reader.

After that, more important things took place over writing; not his family, but his disorder. It grew like wild ivy, filling his skull until it felt like it'd explode at any moment. Repetitive, obsessive thoughts overwhelmed him, a maelstrom of redundancy he couldn't or *wouldn't* pull himself out of. The compulsions controlled every aspect of his life, unheeded by the effect they had on others. It was as though Michael was the thoughts and the thoughts him.

Waking up.

Meals.

Phone calls.

Showering.

Sleeping.

All done exactly at specific and lengths of times, and finished, in

Michael's mind, in order. Not a minute earlier or later. Taking his vitamins *before* brushing his teeth, because who knew what nutrients the mouthwash would kill before reaching his stomach. Dishes cleaned in a rotation of bowls, plates, glasses, then silverware. Dried in the same order, too. Every week on Wednesday he bought the same groceries in the same amount at the same store.

Completing and doing these rituals made him feel secure, balanced, that even though his worth as a member of society had vanished with his income, he at least could ensure that *he* wouldn't, too. If anything interrupted them, anxiety and rage flooded him.

He would be short with Kayla and Aaron, snap at them over every little thing, be *mean* overall; a few times the anger would be so overwhelming he punched a hole in the wall. But the very place that seemed to incite him was the one he was afraid to leave. The outside was unknowable, uncontrollable. Nothing else mattered to him but to feel normal; his routine was the sole way to do that.

Throughout all of this, Kayla kept the family together and afloat by working extra shifts or overtime at the store once she was able to after giving birth. She futilely tried to comprehend what was happening with her husband. But any time Michael attempted to explain to her that he didn't *want* to do these things but *must* do them, they were imperative—like breathing air, drinking water, sleeping—she failed to understand or empathize, and resentment grew, adding to the aggressive outbursts.

So she did what was best for her and their son: a divorce.

He couldn't afford to take care of Aaron, so custody went to her, but he outright refused to give up Zylo. He'd been given as a surprise gift from his mother when he was a teenager. Their pet chihuahua ran away and never returned after a night he wished he could forget. It was as if as quickly as one disappeared, the other appeared, and his dog had been with him ever since.

His mother passed years ago, and his father wasn't and isn't someone he cares to remember. No siblings or distant family he knew of. He only had Zylo and he was *his*, not *hers*. Kayla allowed him to keep him on one condition: He'd go to therapy and start medication. Which he quickly agreed to, for a while.

His key in the front door lock trembles in his grasp. His legs won't move. Inside, the phone rings.

"Come on," he whispers. "Do it."

Turn the fucking key.

Abruptly, he does and shoves the door open before his mind can stop him. Slams it closed behind him. Peering down the hall, flashes of his pet's flitter through his mind: lying outside on the street; the last of his blood spilling out of him when picked up; the lifeless body on the table—

The phone rings.

Trudging through muck—*Ring*—ascending a mountain—*Ring*—crawling across bone-ridden plains—*Ring*—he forces his body forward —*Ring*—and picks up the phone.

"Hello?" he says, dry-mouthed.

"Yes, is this Michael?"

It is.

"Hi, this is Dr. Renar, from Pet General. I was told you had some questions about the autopsy scheduled for your pet."

He did, and asked the ones he had brought up to Mackenzie.

"Without getting into detail, the procedure is quite simple. I thoroughly inspect the animal externally and internally, from their nose and mouth to their rectum. I also run blood work to check for any diseases or deficiencies."

What if he doesn't have any organs? "And how long does this take?"

"A couple hours for the autopsy itself, then about twenty-four to forty-eight hours for the bloodwork."

"Are you able to do DNA tests at all? To see, maybe, if whoever did it left something?"

"I understand the dog was killed—going by the paperwork you filled out earlier—so we can go that route, but we'd have to send it out to have it analyzed, so it'll cost more."

"I'll pay whatever," he says, keeping his sight glued to the wall, not prepared to see the table. "And the results, will you call when you have them? Tell me what took him away."

"Absolutely, we'll have them emailed, too. But I or Mackenzie will call you before then if I need any more information or have questions."

"Thank you, Doctor."

"Welcome," he says, hanging up.

He puts the phone back into its cradle.

You'll have to do it eventually.

The table will always be there.

Could throw it out and buy a new one.

Still would have to look at it, though.

"I know, I know..."

He looks.

Dried blood coats the tabletop, darkened around the rim, and crimson dots the floor. Where he had laid him on the ground, a vague shape of a dog is stained red. Michael breathes in deeply, immediately tastes acidic oatmeal on the back of his tongue. He darts to the sink to retch. Once his stomach is empty, he cleans his face and the basin, then opening the cabinet underneath, he takes out cleaning supplies. No one else can do it, even if he wanted them to.

Zylo was his, after all.

A full trash bag later, the fumes of bleach and soap fill the room, but the blood's gone. He tosses the bag out the back door, and goes upstairs to the bathroom, fighting the compulsion to peer out the stairwell window as he passes, because he has the urge to go out there and clean the pavement, too. He switches the lights on.

I look fucking terrible.

Somehow paler, almost translucent. Cheeks more sunken in, his bones protruding like his pink, burning eyes. When he bares his teeth, his lips crack and bleed. Hair is glued to his scalp by grease and sweat. How hadn't he smelled himself this entire time? He'd been out in public like this. He feels a little bad for anyone who was in his proximity.

"When did I last sleep?"

A day ago, two?

He can't remember, memories overlaid by a surreal film, like oil on water. Grabbing his pills from the medicine cabinet, he downs two dry, then undresses, taking his clothes and the bloody ones from the floor and cramming them into the already full hamper. After the water in the shower gets hot, he gets in.

Michael closes his eyes as it streams over him.

He had seen a therapist for a while, and took the meds prescribed by his psychiatrist. It was a miracle the former was able to break his external compulsions, but his internal ones wouldn't falter, no matter the amount of exercises they tried: CBT, EMDR, ERP, breathing exercises, meditation, working out, diet, new hobbies, new places, new routines.

Seemingly this part of himself was too ingrained into the foundation of who he was, or had always been, and became paramount when he lost his income. And they were unable to determine if the anxiety was what caused the obsessions or vice versa, both likely intertwined since the beginning.

Eventually he concluded the money he was paying for therapy wasn't worth it any longer. By that time he had custody of Zylo already, so there wasn't a point to continue anyway. Michael could function day-to-day, and afford his meager life with unemployment. His relationship with his therapist ended after a year, but the medication stayed.

He wasn't delusional. The meds kept him in check. Without them, he would be organizing the cereal boxes, or counting how long it takes him to brush each side of his teeth before going to another, or he would feel like he can use one cup for everything and if he doesn't...

While the water cooled, fatigue crept into his body. Yawning, he turns off the shower, and grabs a towel from the hook. He dries himself, trudging into his office. Unfinished, doodled-on notes are strewn over the desk, a layer of dust covering the keyboard and monitor. Clean clothes are heaped against the wall beside the computer, copies of his own books lost somewhere underneath. The bedroom is still off-limits, so whatever's in the pile will do. Plain black T-shirt, sweatpants, plaid boxers.

Great.

Wonderful.

After dressing, he goes downstairs and falls face-first onto the couch. Sleep comes quick.

CHAPTER 2

Chiming in the distance, echoing over a vast, dreary field. Each toll brings about pulsating crimson light, radiating through the fog. Mist seeps into the morning sky, revealing the light isn't within the fog, but fissures bolting through the monochrome earth. The light-not-a-light sprays blood. The chiming distorts, changing, transforming into a familiar, electronic ring.

Ring.

Ring.

Ring.

Michael opens his eyes, dry drool on his face.

"Hold on," he mumbles, rolling off the couch. Stumbling as he stands, he half-limps to the phone and wrenches it from the hook.

"Yeah?"

"Michael? This is Dr. Renar, from Pet General."

Drowsiness immediately leaves him. "What happened?"

"I don't know how to word this lightly, it's the first time I've ever seen something like this, frankly. But were you aware of the wounds inside Zylo?"

"No, what sort of wounds?"

"It was something I discovered when we opened him up. There is scarring *inside* his body, but it wasn't the common scar tissue I'd normally expect, if there was any. They were *symbols* or some kind of runes. It had to have been done postmortem, because you couldn't reach inside that deep with the organs present. They're also too precise to not be deliberate."

Runes?

Scars?

What did the sick fuck do to him?

He clenches his teeth, shaking his head. "No, I don't know anything about it."

"Okay, I just wanted to speak to you before you received the autopsy, which includes photographs of the scarring. I didn't want it to be a surprise or anything like that, because it was to me." He awkwardly chuckles.

"Thanks, is the autopsy done?"

"Yes, but we're still waiting for the analysts on some things, like the hair you gave us, which should be a couple days, tops. You may receive the autopsy by email before someone has the chance to call you. But I have to go—do you have any other questions?"

Michael doesn't, so they say their goodbyes, and he hangs up the phone.

Glancing at the clock, he realizes he had slept well over fourteen hours. "It's...Friday?" His belly grumbles, but he's too pissed to eat. *I need to find out who did this. He needs to be put in jail or given the chair or the fucking guillotine.*

"Should I call the police?"

No. Willow or Wallah or whatever his name is obviously doesn't care, neither did that receptionist.

But what can he do? He doesn't have the faintest idea of who could do this, or that it was even one person—it could've been a group. Michael doesn't have the power the police have, or the money, or any sort of leads pointing him in the right direction. He's a writer—well, *was*—not a cop or a detective or PI.

Meandering to the sink, he stares into the neighbor's yard. Their white terrier sits in the grass, barking at the house, its shaggy hair brown at the ends. Must've been playing in the mud. Michael smiles, frowns. Zylo loved rolling around in the dirt, especially after it rained. He *hated* baths, though.

"This sucks."

He paces around the kitchen in a circle until finally his gnawing stomach is too annoying to tolerate and makes a peanut butter and banana sandwich. Eats. Still hungry. Eats another. Considers a third but he doesn't want to get *too* full.

"What the hell do I do?" he asks no one.

When I wrote and hit a wall in the story, what did I do to solve it?

Murder isn't a plot hole. They're nothing alike.

The back of his head aches.

"Okay, okay... If I was writing a book *now* about someone in my position, what would I do first?"

Well, I'd look up stuff online.

The internet.

Michael runs upstairs, plugs in the Ethernet cord, boots up the computer, curses himself for thinking of this sooner.

He stares at the dusted-off screen with his fingers glued to the keyboard, unsure of what to search. *Dead dogs, disemboweled dogs, organs cut out of dogs,* and others run through his mind, but he's wary of searching for those and being bombarded with horrendous photos he never wants to witness in his life. He's seen some awful things online before, especially in his spam folder, but in Michael's state, a photo like that would send him reeling. He's now appreciative that the vet had called him before sending over everything.

"But I have to," he says, and types, slowly: *Dog murdered.* Before pressing enter: *Rune scars.*

Photos appear at the top but he quickly scrolls down to the articles. Surprisingly, there's more than he expected. All with similar titles: *Stray Dog Found Cut Open at Palinksi Park; Utah Man's Dog Murdered in Front of His Home; 12-Year-Old's Newly Adopted Pet Discovered Brutally Murdered.* In spite of not wanting to look at or read the stories of all these poor, undeserving animals taken away from the world, he clicks on the articles, opening each into new tabs in the web browser. He skips some, choosing a few at random. Once they're loaded, he pulls the Ethernet from the phone jack, just in case someone calls, and begins reading.

He skims, searching for specific terms in the hopes some piece of Zylo's puzzle will appear.

"Dada...dada...dada... *German Shepherd found without innards in Salem, Massachusetts... No leads, but the police are investigating...*" Dated two months ago. No updates. *The police there must do as much as they do here. Figures.*

On to the next.

"All the 70-year-old woman, Debrah Katsner, had left in her life was Nala, her ten-year-old Rat Terrier. But now, that's been taken away, too... The dog was found outside her home, cut open, and missing its organs... She decided against an autopsy..." Dated six months ago. Somewhere in Missouri. No leads or updates. No mention of scars or runes.

Next.

"...Humphrey, his German Shepherd, was discovered without organs by the volunteer fire department in Lititz, Pennsylvania... The owner, who asked to remain anonymous, has allowed us to share the results of the autopsy he had done, in the hopes that it will help catch whoever did this... We're not going to go into the grisly details, but Humphrey was without organs and scars covered the inside of his body..."

Scars. Not runes, but scars. Article's a year old, but Michael finds the journalist's email and copies it into a text document with the URL to the article.

...

A 32-year-old woman in California's Shih Tzu was discovered cut open in front of the police station. Scars in the shape of symbols found within. Dated two years ago. Michael notes the journalist's email and the URL.

...

A couple's Rottweiler in Boulder, Colorado was discovered Saturday morning murdered on their front porch, still tied to its leash. It was on its back, revealing abnormal scarring. Dated four years ago. Michael notes and copies.

...

A 65-year-old man's Italian Greyhound found murdered and without organs...strange iconography in its insides. Dated three months ago. Notes, copies.

...

The world recedes into the aether as Michael delves through the horrors. It feels as though he's no longer in his chair, in his office, in his home, in his body. Floating in the abyss, just him and the computer, the screen's dim blue glow illuminating his pale face. One story after another containing unspeakable acts made against the most innocent creatures, all across the country.

Soon, he discovers it's not solely in the US but in Europe, Canada, Germany. Whoever's doing this has been at it for years, all over the globe. Michael isn't sure if it's intentional, but they seem to put enough time and distance between each murder to not raise red flags with the police. But he's certain all of this is too much for one person alone.

Has to be a group, a fucking cult or something harvesting animal organs.

"But why? For what?"

Deeper down the rabbit hole. There's too many articles, too many mentions of canine corpses and scars or symbols, the evidence piling up to the point Michael has over twenty URLs with email addresses of all the journalists.

It's obvious what's happening. What happened to his pup. He wasn't chosen specifically. It was random. He happened to be at the wrong place at the wrong time when they rolled through town. Could've been the neighbors' dog, if he'd been out front. Michael imagines a group of black-clad men in a van seeing Zylo in the front yard, likely pissing on the side of the house or staring across the street; they barrel out of an open sliding door, holding him down as he tries to fight them off, his dark eyes growing wide and glossy as the bite of a box cutter—

"No!"

Michael pushes himself away from the computer like it burns him, the void around him cast away. He shoves his face into his hands and sobs, chest racking, lungs burning. Michael wishes he could liquefy and sink into his palms, as though a nothingness is beneath flesh and bone; a place without hurt, pain, where Zylo would be, where his brain worked like a normal person's and he wouldn't be where he is now, alone, in a room meant to be his workspace but is closer to a dresser drawer than anything else.

Sitting up and sharply inhaling through a clogged nose, he uses the back of his hand to clean his eyes and mouth. Then, he hears something: The phone's ringing.

"Michael, you have Aaron today, remember?" Kayla says. "From four to nine."

"I, ah... Yeah, I remember," he lies, wanting to get back to the computer. The information has been the only possible lead to finding Zylo's *killers*. Plural. Though it probably won't come to much, Michael also needs to call Wollah and tell him what he's found. Also, he should look online about cults, or maybe go to the library. Maybe after he gets the report from the vet and knows what the symbols look like he'll make better progress.

"...I'll be dropping him off soon. Okay?"

Shit. Has she been talking all this time?

"That works."

"Sorry, I haven't asked in a while, since I hate doing it, but have you been taking your meds?"

"Daily."

"And what about therapy?"

"Every week."

To Michael, Aaron's the perfect blend of Kayla and him. He has Michael's dark eyes and strong jaw, and Kayla's soft brown hair and smooth skin. He hopes he hasn't gotten their short height gene. Either way, the girls and/or boys, Michael couldn't say which way his son may lean, will have a field day once he's grown up.

They stand in the entry, Aaron bundled in a blue winter coat and sweats, taking off his boots on the bottom step of the stairwell. Kayla wears thick eye shadow and liner, her hair moussed and spiked in the back, lips painted dark, and silver-studded earrings hang from her dainty lobes. She smells like marshmallows roasting over an open fire.

"Where're you heading?" he says, glancing at Aaron, back to her.

"Just going out," she says. "Nothing crazy."

Despite their separation, a twinge of jealousy resonates deep inside Michael. He knows he shouldn't feel like this after this long, but he does. The question "With who?" hovers in his mind. But ultimately, it's better for him to not know too much and not pry.

Aaron tears off the other boot and sets both by the wall. Kayla crouches in front of him, holding his shirt collar, and says, "Now you be a good boy for your dad. He's got lots of fun things planned while I'm gone." She side-eyes him. "Don't you?"

"Oh," he says, on cue, "absolutely. So many things. Strippers, booze, guns; the whole shebang."

She rolls her eyes, then faces Aaron. "Now give Mommy a hug."

He wraps his small arms around her neck, and she embraces him as though she'll never see him again. Kisses him on the cheek before straightening.

"Nine o'clock, Michael. I'll be back on the dot."

Aaron gets to his feet from the step and comes over to him. Michael rubs the back of his head, and puts his hand on his shoulder. "Got it."

She waves, says "love you" to Aaron, and leaves, closing the door behind her.

His son glances around, and looks up at him. He meets his gaze. "Dad, where's Zylo?"

"He..." It's like a punch in the gut, grief bubbling up, but he forces it down and smiles. A kid shouldn't know things like this yet, even Michael knows that. "Didn't your mom tell you about him?"

"No, what?"

That... How could she not tell him about him by now? How could she let him come here knowing that he's gone when every time he comes over, he tackles him to the ground and licks his face until I pull him off.

How could she dump this on me while I'm dealing with finding his killers? She did say she wouldn't mention it, but you'd think she'd make up an excuse before bringing him here... Fucking hell—

He hides the frustration in his voice. "He went away, Aaron."

"Where'd he go?"

Michael crouches to his son's height. "He...went to work for the police."

"The police!" He jumps, hands clenched. "Is he going to catch bad guys?"

"Absolutely, he is. Best dog they ever got, the police chief said."

A few tears come unnoticed. *Shit.* Aaron deflates, and wipes his father's cheek. "Why're you crying, Dad?"

"Just miss him, that's all."

Aaron wraps his arms around him, and he embraces him. He feels too small, something that could be easily broken. A hint of Kayla's smokey, sweet perfume lingers on him. "Don't worry. We can see him later, right?"

"One day, maybe," he whispers into his hair. "If he's not too busy catching all those bad guys."

Aaron doesn't reply, so silently they hold each other until Michael breaks away, standing. "All right, let's get some pizza."

"Can I get any kind I want?"

"You can get anything you want, bud."

After the pizza's delivered, they sit in the living room and eat from paper plates. A television show he didn't catch the name of plays in the background, but it captivates Aaron like nothing else, his eyes glued to the TV. Although it's uncomfortable, like a coat two sizes too small, like an extra layer of flesh that won't stop moving, Michael does what he ought to do. Something his therapist reiterated in countless sessions.

Communicate. Engage with his loved ones. Get out of his head.

"So how's school?"

"Good," Aaron says, mouth half full with pizza.

"Learn anything cool?"

He shakes his head. "Uh-huh."

"Have any friends?"

"Some, yeah. Tommy, Nathan, Tyler..."

"You guys hang out? Ride bikes or something?"

"Mom won't let me have a bike." He wipes his face with a napkin.

"Wha— Why not?"

"Says I'll fall and get hurt."

For some reason, this gets under Michael's skin. A tinge of flabbergasted annoyance. *She won't let her son ride a bike? At his age?* When Michael was that old all he did was ride his bike around the neighborhood, even in winter. Met other kids who did the same. Made friends. Spent days messing around back behind the high school with makeshift ramps, and riding through the small stretch of woods between the parking lot and baseball fields. Countless weeks, months, creating memories that made him long for his youth before the world inevitably crushed him.

"Well, maybe Santa will get you one this year for Christmas."

Aaron finishes his slice and grabs another from the box on the table. The show goes to commercial. "Tommy says Santa's not real."

"Tommy's a liar," Michael spits in a knee-jerk reaction. "Santa's as real as you and me." The bike's one thing, but the magical wonderment of the belief in Santa's something wholly different. He refuses to allow his kid to have his Christmas ruined by disbelief, at least, not until he's older. Another thing of his youth he cherishes and wishes he could return to, but more importantly, he wants Aaron to experience, too.

"Okay." Aaron shrugs, and keeps eating.

By seven, Aaron's asleep on the couch, pizza sauce smeared on his cheek. Drool trickles from his open mouth.

Michael gathers the leftovers and plates, shoving the food in the fridge for Aaron to take with him later and the plates in the bin. He creeps upstairs to the computer. He plugs the internet back in, and wakes up the monitor, revealing where he had left off.

"Enough of that." He closes the web articles. His text document has eighteen reports of similar dog murders around the globe within the last decade or so. Instead, he searches *dog runes*, taking him to a few websites about Norse symbology and ways of spelling "dog" in runic text, but not much else. What images there are illustrate stories from Norse mythology, which is great if that's what he was looking for, but the screen captures and photographs of runic memorabilia, or merchandise from a variety of online stores, are of absolutely no interest.

Micheal groans. "Nothing."

There's a knock on the door. *Is that her already?* He checks the time: 9:01 p.m. *It's already nine? Damn.* Michael hurries downstairs to wake Aaron up, then gets the door.

"You're late," he says.

"By one minute," Kayla says, coming inside.

She reeks of cigarette smoke and beer, but her breath is minty. Michael didn't know she's become the bar type, recalling vividly she preferred coffee shops and quiet restaurants when they went out. At least he knows her well enough to know he doesn't have to worry about her drinking and driving. She's always been the smarter one in the marriage.

After Michael helps Aaron gather his things, his son gets his boots on.

"So how was it?" Kayla says.

"It was fun," Aaron says.

"Yeah," Michael chips in, "it was a blast."

"What'd you guys do?"

Aaron works on his laces. "Watched TV, had pizza— Mom!"

"What is it?"

"Did you know that Zylo works for the police now?" He finishes the bunny ears on his shoes, and stands. "He's gonna catch bad guys!"

Kayla stares at Michael, whose lips are drawn tight. "Yeah, Kayla," he says, "did you know that?"

She mouths: "I'm so sorry," then: "Yeah, I did, honey. Now tell your dad goodbye, it's time to go."

Michael crouches as Aaron comes over and they hug. "Love you, Dad."

"You too, bud."

After they drive away, taillights vanishing into the night, he closes the door. Instantly, the weighty, uneasy silence of the empty house is all too well-known.

"Should I make some coffee and keep going?"

He's hit a wall again, but not one he can get around. It feels like he hasn't done enough, isn't *doing* enough, as if he's given up.

There isn't much I can do without the autopsy.

So the work must stop temporarily, no matter how much he wants to go on or how guilty he feels. It's out of his hands.

Turning off the downstairs lights, he crashes on the couch. Thoughts ricochet in his skull, but an inkling that he forgot something surfaces. He can't quite place it with everything else blaring in his mind. He's sure he did all that he needed to do that day, so it couldn't be that important.

Eventually, his mind wanes and sleep comes.

CHAPTER 3

After adjusting the boxes of cereal in the cabinet a few times, Michael goes into his office with a cup of coffee. The computer screen awakens, a notification at the top of his email inbox: *1 New Email*.

He sets his mug aside as he opens his inbox. It's from Pet General, and clicking it open, it's blank besides two attachments: a scan of the autopsy and photographs of Zylo's internal scars. Wiping his clammy palms on his pants doesn't help. The autopsy reveals nothing that he was hoping for. No DNA besides his pups. No fingerprints or hair fibers besides Michael's. No semen or foreign substances, nor any other blood types. No drugs or alcohol in his system. He did die just from the murder.

He takes a deep shuddering breath, putting his focus to the images. He opens them in their own individual browser windows. They're black and white and poor quality, but enough to make out the—not scars or symbols, but *runes*.

"The vet was right."

They scatter across his insides like constellations in the night sky. Some are too tiny to see, others big and clearly visible. Michael doesn't know what any of them mean in the slightest.

"Who would do something like this?" he says for the hundredth time.

Running his finger over the convex glass, he follows the runic quilt blanketing Zylo. A few Michael likens to F and R—maybe a vertical Z? A couple could be intertwining S's within a circle pronged with pitchforks. There's one used many times, more of a drawing than a letter. Crude, jagged lines like two overlapping sets of minimalistic drawn mountains below a large circle.

His temples ache staring at the screen, eyes dry and stinging, so he prints out the autopsy report, the photos, some of the news articles, and his notes with all the URLs and emails. Despite wanting to figure out the runes himself, solve the mystery, and understand the medical report; he's aware Wollah should take a look at it first, regardless of his uselessness. The police usually have professionals who can help with this sort of thing, and point Michael in the right direction before he follows the wrong one.

Michael gathers everything, chugs his now-cold coffee, and gets dressed.

It's snowing more before he gets to the station by bus. His cheeks and lips burn, and his nose refuses to stop running. He already can't feel his fingers. *Should've worn more layers.* At the front desk, the same secretary from a couple days ago sits behind the plexiglass. She reads from another TV guide. He knocks on the glass. She sighs, keeping the book open with a thumb as she faces him.

"Hello, again."

"Hi—is Wollah in now?"

"Lemme check." She puts the phone to her ear and pokes the numbers in its cradle.

"Hi, Tim, it's Susan out front. Sorry to bother you, but there's a man here who wants to talk to you. Hold on." She covers the receiver. "What're you here for?"

"About my dog. He came to my house a few days ago." *Has it been days? Or a week?* Michael can't remember.

"He says about a dog," she says into the phone. "Says you went to his house. Yeah, okay. Will do. Thanks, Tim." She hangs up. "Go through there." She points to an opaque plexiglass door off to the side. "His office is number three, second on the right." She presses a button, a buzzer sounds, and the door seemingly unlocks.

"Thank you."

Down a gray-blue carpeted hall with hanging framed photos of officers posing in front of the US flag on the wood-paneled wall, he comes to #3 and knocks.

"Come in."

Inside matches the hallway, except for a dark green filing cabinet in the corner, a desk taking up most of the space, Wollah behind it, and an empty chair against the wall.

"Close it."

He does, and stands in front of the desk. "I got more information about my dog, Zylo."

Wollah reclines, runs a hand through his thinning hair. "Ah, yeah, the dog. What do you think you have?"

Michael sets down the paper-clipped notes, autopsy, and images. He's aware the officer may think he's insane, knowing what he's about to say will probably be shooting himself in the foot, but it's the truth. It's what he wholeheartedly believes. "There's a group of people killing dogs, cutting runes into them, and stealing their organs for some reason." Sweat runs down his back. He regrets not putting on deodorant. "It's been happening for a decade, or maybe longer."

The cop gazes at Michael, who doesn't look away. "Are you being serious?"

He nods, unclips the papers, and spreads them out across the desk, ignoring what work Wollah was doing before. "Look, the photos of the scars, the autopsy report; here's articles about similar killings, and this is a list of like twenty others, with dates and emails of all the journalists. All happening around the world."

The officer sits up and adjusts his baby-blue dress shirt. Wollah scans the news articles, flips through the photos, skims the autopsy, runs a finger down the list. "These go back ten years, and only twenty-something dog killings? Nothing unusual found in the lab work. Don't have much to go on here."

Michael rubs his forehead. "True, but it's the way they're done. What's it called, MO?"

"Even if fifty dogs were killed in the same way in a decade, without a connection between them, you ain't got shit. If I looked on the computer right now about animals killed by shovels, I'm sure I'd find double this in the same time frame. And the runes or whatever, they're *strange*, but I'm sure it's not mentioned in every one of these articles, are they?"

"More than half—"

Wollah whistles. "If this all happened within a couple years, I'd say you have something, but with this..." He shakes his head. "You can't really prove anything except there's a bunch of nut-jobs in the world, not some sort of dog-killing, organ-stealing club."

Maybe he's right, maybe I'm seeing what I want to see.

Trying to make sense of what happened.

Slotting pieces into a puzzle, even if there isn't a puzzle at all.

But I feel it in every fiber of my being that I'm right...

This guy wouldn't help before, why would he help now? He doesn't care about me, Zylo, about anything since it's not a human who died. I could bring the killer into his office, have him admit what he did, and Wollah would have an excuse why it wasn't the killer, and I should let him go. Or they'd just slap him with the useless fine and he'd be back out on the street in a couple hours.

"So are you going to have the report looked at by the medical examiner or something?" he says as a Hail Mary. "Or follow up with the journalists?"

The officer chuckles. "I can look over it some more, but I think you're jumping the gun a bit. The ME won't look at anything unless it's very important, he's busy as it is with an overflow from Cherry Brooke. *Maybe* email some of the folks you got there." He collects the papers and stacks them, setting them aside. "But I'll get straight to the point. It's only a dog—one dog among millions of others, but millions of *people* need our help more."

Only a dog?

Only a fucking dog?

Michael shoves his hands in his pockets to hide squeezing them.

He was Zylo.

My best friend.

My everything.

Animals are pure innocence, they don't know shit but love and devotion, unless abused by useless bastards, like you. Any dog owner understands and knows they're not just pets; they're far more than that.

Michael quells the urge to leap over the desk. "Thanks," he seethes. "I'll call you in a week or two for updates. Is that okay?"

Wallah nods. "I'll be here."

He leaves the office, not shutting the door, and strides down the hall into the lobby. Out the front doors, the frigid air cuts into him, but he barely feels it, the boiling anger keeping the chill from rooting deeper.

Michael rounds the corner a block away, turns into a vacant alley, and screams. His fists collide with the red brick wall, and his feet smash against a dumpster, ringing hollowly. He runs his numb fingers through his hair, clenches a clump, and screams again, lungs burning with winter. His labored breath comes out as fog.

"I can't—I can't rely on them, *him.*"

His arms dangle to his sides, fatigued. His fingers and toes sting either from his outburst or the cold or both, and his knuckles bleed, bits of grit in the wounds. He leans back against the wall and lets gravity take him to the ground. Michael shakes his head, arms propped on his knees, snowflakes melting in his hair.

I have to do what I've been saying since the start of all this.

"I'll have to find them myself."

Taking a beat, he finally gets up. His hands hurt and he realizes he broke a few of his nails. Dull pain radiates through his feet. Inhaling deeply, the air cooling the simmering anger, he makes his way to the nearest bus stop.

White opaques the kitchen window, the first blizzard of the year. The coffee pot percolates. The vents blow hot air, and Michael tries to not think about how Zylo used to sit in front of the one in his bedroom. Michael adjusts the chair to the left.

So, a plan.

"First..." Moves the chair to the right. *I shouldn't be doing this.* "I need to contact some of the journalists, and see if anyone can help me."

Or should I try to figure out what the rune means first?

To the left a little. He shakes his head, curses, and attempts to let go of the chair but fails. The coffee pot hisses, an aroma of hazelnut filling the room. He wishes he could have some now.

"Maybe... But wouldn't that be jumping the gun? Wollah might be right. I could be wasting my time. I need to contact them to see if what happened to Zylo is what happened to them. They could already have some stuff figured out, or tell me where to go next."

Right. "Fuck."

Left. *Closer.*

Contact journalists, cross-reference the murders, then what?

"Depends on what I get from them. If things match up and I still don't know anything about the runes, the next step is to figure those out. Feel like they're the key to all this bullshit. But if they give me something to work off of, I might be able to move onto finding out who the killers are."

Right.

Left.

Michael tastes success. *It's only a chair. There's no winning here.* His jaw tenses. *I could be working on figuring shit out already, closer to an actual goal than this.* His knuckles whiten.

Right, a teensy bit.

Left.

Tension builds in his shoulders, climbing his neck. *It's pointless, a dumb thing my head does. I could throw the chair across the room and it'll make the same difference where it's at now.* His eyes furrow. *I'll still be here if I let go.* Again, he fails, stomach clenching.

Right.

Left.

Stops.

"There," he sighs with relief, the world lifting from his shoulders. His fingers ache when he lets go, and it feels like he can breathe again. Michael knows he shouldn't feel the way he does for what he did, some semblance of short-lived pride and accomplishment flooding him, but it's there nonetheless. *I'll try better next time.* "Now time for coffee."

Without any available outlets in the office and no extra extension cords, Michael lugs the computer and printer down into the kitchen. It'll be convenient to be able to type and talk at the same time. He makes a mental note to buy more cords at some point.

Before disconnecting the internet, he goes through the articles he has noted and writes down the phone numbers he can find on the websites. Emails are sent to journalists asking about their articles, the killings, attaching photos of Zylo's runes in the hopes that alone will spark an interest for them to help him. With a list of nearly twenty numbers, he plugs the phone back in, opens a text document, and begins.

"Hello, yes, my name's Michael and I'm from Carlysle City, Pennsylvania. I'd like to ask you about..."

"Hey, my name's Michael. I'm from Pennsylvania, and I'd like to speak to you..."

"Oh, sorry; must've got the wrong number. Do you have the number for..."

"Hey, I'm Michael, from Pennsylvania. Can I talk to you..."

"My name's Michael. I'm calling about..."

His voice, the mechanical click of the keyboard, the humming of the computer, fills the silence for what feels like forever, interrupted only by eating when it's eleven a.m. and six p.m., refreshing the coffee, and going to the bathroom. Wind howls against the house, white piles on his front porch, against the door, and small dunes form in the yard. Night fades to morning. Faintly he hears the clang of the metal mailbox closing, the neighbor's terrier barking to be let in, the snow plow going down the street every couple hours.

The phone numbers he begins with spawn a dozen more, then another dozen. Everyone seemingly has another person he could contact, *if* he needs more information. Yet almost all of them are dead ends, especially from the journalists of the articles posted years ago.

"No, of course I don't recall..."

"It's been ten years! How do you expect me to remember that?"

"Runes? What the hell are you talking about? Are you sure you got the right number?"

"Thanks for reminding me, jackass..."

"...can't you just leave well enough alone?"

Michael slams down the phone and cradles his head in his hands. His eyes keep burning when he shuts them, and the monitor's light ebbs in dull yellows and reds across the black of his eyelids.

That many people and not a fucking thing.

"I've wasted so much time."

Opening his eyes and yawning, something rancid burns the back of his throat. He grimaces. *Must be from the coffee.*

The phone rings, and he immediately picks up.

"Hi, Michael? It's Dr. Renar, just following up about your animal's autopsy. You received it in an email already, right?"

He groans. *Fucking Christ, right now?* "Yeah."

"I'm sure you've already went through it, but I'd like to cover—"

"I already know what I needed from it. I don't need any more help."

"Are you sure?"

"I wouldn't have said it if I wasn't."

"Well, okay, but—"

Michael hangs up and tears the landline out, shoving in the internet cable. *Emails. Have to get to the emails.* The screeching, chittering electronic noise grates on his warm ears until abruptly ending. He rubs his forehead, opening his email inbox.

Ten responses.

Michael cracks his neck, stretches his arms and rotates his wrists.

"Here we go again."

By the time he finishes going through the emails it's night again. He comes to the same end he reached with the phone calls: Nowhere. Some have automatic responses stating the email address no longer exists or is in service. Some are responded to by someone else, who apparently works at the newspaper or website, saying that the person he's trying to contact no longer works there, they don't have a forwarding address, and they have no information about the article or the runes.

All others are unreplied to. There *are* two responded to by actual journalists: one retired who has no memory of "the dog thing"; the other is fuzzy on the details and has no time to go through it again, but she does wish Michael good luck with his venture, though.

Michael's too beat to be upset. *It is what it is.* Defeated, he switches off the monitor, puts the phone line back in, and takes his dirty dishes heaped on the table and dumps them into the sink. Turns on the hot water. Through a small, clear patch of the window, the neighbor's back-door light illuminates a dog chain lying on the shoveled ground.

Vividly, he recalls Zylo's first heavy snow, before Aaron was born. At the open back door, excitement ran through Michael and Kayla. He couldn't stop smiling, and she kept giggling. Zylo stood just before the doorway, staring outside with his head tilted. He raised a paw as though wanting to test the waters, then he'd set it down, raise it, set it down.

"C'mon, boy," he said. "It's just snow." He picked up a handful. "See?"

Zylo tip-tapped a little, leaned back, forward. Neared the door. Wind blew flakes into the house. The floor rumbled as the heat kicked on. "He better hurry up," Kayla said, "or our bill is going to be through the roof."

"Come on, you can do it."

He barked, and cautiously stepped into the snow. Stood for a second like registering what the white fluff covering his paws was. Then he took off, zooming across the yard, barely visible with how high the snow was. He tried to leap over a mound by the garage but made it halfway, falling into it. A second later he burst out from it and ran some more. He dug his head randomly into the white, searching for God knew what.

Michael quickly got his winter gear on, joining Zylo. He jogged alongside him, tossed snowballs for him to catch, which confused him when they melted in his mouth. Michael made snow angels while his pup had zoomies around him, all the while Kayla watched from the door, laughing so hard she had tears in her eyes.

I miss them.

The hot water in the sink drowns the dirty dishes and he turns it off.

Letting them soak, he goes to lie down for the night. *After I wake up, I have to go to the library. They'll know something there. Librarians know everything.*

The next afternoon, Michael prints out an image of the symbols. He puts on two long-sleeve T-shirts under his coat, a pair of sweatpants under faded black jeans, and two pairs of socks. In front of the house, he collects all the mail from the box, and what fell on the porch. He curses himself for not getting around to buying gloves, fingers numb, tossing it all by the vent in the entryway.

Deal with that later.

He catches the bus at the corner, and grabs a seat by the window. The shift in the weather doesn't change the town, no different than it was. Smokestacks billow thick smoke into the gray sky, restaurants stand stoically, their parking lots icy and salted; people bundled in hats, scarves, jackets, and boots trudge down the sidewalk, wincing and bracing against the wind. The abandoned buildings seem sadder, drift collecting against them, trickling through broken windows.

Downtown, he gets off close by the Carlysle City Public Library. Michael hasn't been there since he was a child, but the looming, dark brown brick building looks the same. *Like a monolithic block of clay with big square windows.* A short set of stairs leads to an area under a wide awning with metal benches along the far wall, littered with debris and trash.

The warmth inside is heavenly, and he stands by the entry's heater a moment before entering the building proper. Making his way to the holiday-decorated dark wood counter in the center, his boots squeak on the granite floor. No one's there. Michael rings a rusted bell on the desk, and scans his surroundings. Towering shelves line every available space, freestanding cases throughout on the gray-blue carpet, replacing granite, and people hunch at computers in the back.

"Sir?" a woman says from behind.

He turns. Gold-rimmed glasses sit on her small nose, shielding blue eyes. Her graying auburn hair done in a bun, bangs hair-clipped behind her ears. "Hi, I'm wondering if you have any books that deal with... runes, I guess. Symbols."

"What kind? Norse? Pagan? There's many types."

Michael takes out the photo and hands it to her. "Something like this."

She props her glasses up with her finger. "These look more Norse. At least to me, but I'm no expert." She sets aside the printout and faces the computer. "I think we have some books that could help, but we don't carry much."

Unsure if she's talking to him or to herself, he nods anyway.

"Ah, there we go." The enormous printer next to the monitor whirls to life and slowly spews out paper. She tears it from the top tray, handing it to Michael. "Here's a list of what we have. They all fall in the same category, so they can be found in the back." She points. "And if you have any more questions, I'd be happy to help you."

"I will," he says. "Thanks."

"The internet is so much easier," Michael whispers, looking from the paper to the shelves. There's only three books on the list, but it's like trying to find a needle in a haystack. He already has one tucked under his arm, a large hardback, but the other two are nowhere to be found. At the end of the aisle, he rereads the paper, then the little white sign jutting from the top of the bookcase.

"Yup, right place..." He doubles back. *There it is.* He plucks a thick paperback from the top shelf, puts it under his arm, and continues. Crouching, he slowly skims the bindings... "Finally." He removes a thin book squished between two encyclopedias.

Michael picks an empty table to sit at and spreads out the three books and the photo of the inner scars. He leafs through the first book —*Runelore: The Magic, History, and Hidden Codes of the Runes*. It gives a lot of detailed information about runes and their esoteric history, but no mention or photo of the double mountains within a circle. And his photo, Michael realizes, is too grainy to discern which rune is which, *except* for the mountain one, when comparing them to the contents in *Runelore*.

Grumbling, he sets the book aside, opens the hardback—*The Old*

English Rune Poem—and quickly discovers it to be an in-depth analysis of runic poetry written during the Viking Age. It reads more like a required textbook he'd need in college than anything else.

He sets it on the other, and grabs the last book. It's flimsy and the glossy cover is frayed along the edges. "*Nordic Runes: Symbology, Religion, and Faith,*" he says, opening it. Michael already believes he isn't going to find what he's searching for. *If the last two books, which were very thorough on the subject, had nothing, why would this one?* Michael rests his head in his hand while the other flips through the book.

Nope.

Turns page.

Nope.

Turns page.

Nope.

Turns page.

Nope—"Wait."

He puts his printout next to the symbol at the bottom of the page. The jagged mountains, the circle... "Holy shit."

The symbol's name, *Svulek,* is written in small text and underneath, in smaller text, reads: *Created by the Følgere av Fenrir (Followers of Fenrir) in the thirteenth century (turn to pg. 82 for more information).* Heart racing, he goes to page eighty-two. The *Svulek* is at the top above a couple paragraphs speaking about the Followers of Fenrir. He rechecks his picture against what's there, to ensure he's not hallucinating.

He's not.

"*The Followers of Fenrir originated in the thirteen century...*

"*...Their sigil, the* Svulek, *represents the fangs of Fenrir devouring what's believed to be, the sun, moon, or the world. It's unknown what specifically the circle represents.*

"*...Much is not known about the Followers. Some believe they were a religious sect beginning sometime before or during the Scottish-Norwegian Conflict in 1262, stemming from the Forkynner av Æsir (Harbingers of Aesir).*

"*...The group fell into obscurity by the end of the thirteenth century, most scholars believe from a lack of faith and following.*"

Michael sits back.

The Followers of Fenrir... Is it a group killing animals and just using the symbol for shock value? Like what happened in the '80s during the Satanic Panic? Pentagrams on walls in red paint, 666 scrawled across abandoned houses, black candles, occult books, and other "Satanic" things that were done by insane people and not by actual Satanists?

"Or do they still exist today, and no one's paying attention?"

What the hell did I find?

Michael's legs don't feel like his own when he stands. Everything is surreal, as though he slipped into another reality slightly off-kilter from his. It reminds him of when his anxiety is so overwhelming his mind dissociates. He's there, but not. His fingers fumble over *Nordic Runes* as he gathers it, leaving the other two on the table. Someone will get them eventually. At the counter, he carefully sets the book down in front of the librarian.

"Do you know if you have anything else on this?" It takes effort to get the words out as he opens to the *Svulek*.

She leans forward, scans the text. "I don't believe so. Never seen that before. You'll have better luck at the city's public library or museum, even."

The thought of having to go into the city makes him inwardly recoil. "Can you scan this page, please?"

"Certainly." She takes the book and disappears behind a bookshelf. He hears a door open and close.

Followers of Fenrir... Christ.

How'd the Fenrir story go?

Something about biting off a hand, being chained to a rock...

He was the son of Loki and some kind of giant...

The librarian returns, handing him the paper. "Is that all for today?"

"Yeah, thank you. I appreciate it," he says, and walks as quickly as he can to the bus stop.

A steaming cup by his side, the skin of an orange on a napkin, he scratches his forehead as he hunches over the keyboard, reading the myth of Fenrir. There are too many damn names and Michael keeps getting lost.

"He was the son of the god Loki and the giantess Angerboda." He says aloud, lessening the confusion. "The gods were afraid of him because he was so big, and feared he would destroy the Nine Worlds. After failing to chain him twice with iron chains, they had dwarves forge a magical chain, Gleipnir, made from the sound of a cat's footfall, women's beard, roots of the mountains, bear sinew, a fish's breath, and bird spit."

Gross.

"But Fenrir refused the chain unless one of the gods would stick their hand in his mouth, pledging good faith that he'd be freed. Tyr volunteered. Once Fenrir couldn't break the chain, and learned he *wouldn't* be freed, he tore Tyr's hand from his arm. A sword was used to keep his jaw closed, and he was left imprisoned until Ragnarok. When Ragnarok comes, he will break free and devour the world."

Other websites have different interpretations of the story, but it seems the story's foundation is roughly the same.

"So what's this got to do with killing dogs?"

He searches *Followers of Fenrir*, but only more articles about Fenrir or Norse mythology come up. Michael sits back, sighing. His eyes ache, matching his lower back. He doesn't understand. *What's the point of it? Kill dogs to do what? Summon Fenrir? Is this what these idiots believe they're doing? And how are they around today? They're so obscure, even back then, how could they still be a group now?*

"And they don't even have a website."

What do I do now?

The question weighs upon him. He's made progress, knowing, sort of, who took Zylo, but it leads to another wall. Even when he goes into the city, all he'll probably learn is more about Fenrir. He'd be surprised if the Followers are mentioned in anything he finds.

He taps his fingers on the table. The back of his head pounds.

He'd be stupid to believe he'll get an address or someone in the city who could point him in their direction. *Do they even operate out of PA, in the US? Is it just one group, or are they like churches, one at every corner? For all I know they could've been passing through town to some weird cult party and decided to kill him on a whim.*

It feels as if his skeleton yearns to burst from its flesh prison and run away from all of this. From what, though? And where would it go? He doesn't know. Groaning, he sits forward, elbows propped up on bobbing knees.

"Getting ahead of yourself, Michael."

Slowly he breathes in, out, in, out... His legs stop shaking. "Okay, okay... Do what you know and deal with the rest of it when it comes. Freaking out now doesn't help."

He faces the monitor again, and searches for bus times from Carlysle City to Cherry Brooke.

The following morning, Michael has breakfast at seven a.m., finishing his coffee before taking his vitamins, gargles mouthwash, then brushes his teeth. He dresses in multiple layers before going downstairs to gather his notes into a wrinkled manila folder he doesn't remember owning. As he puts his shoes on in the entry, someone knocks at the door.

"Hold on!"

He finishes tying the knot, and opens the door to a wide-shouldered man wearing a brown coat and slacks, carrying a small package and standing on his porch. "Are you Michael Green?"

"Yeah."

"Sign this." He puts the package under his arm and holds out a clipboard with a form pinned to the top. Michael scribbles something resembling his name, and the man quickly gives him the box. While the delivery man strides back to his van, Michael closes the door with his foot. At the kitchen table, he cuts away the tape with a knife, and tears apart the cardboard and Styrofoam inside.

A small creamy-brown wooden box is within and, beneath it, a note:

Greetings Mr. Green,

Zylo was cared for throughout the cremation process, and we're terribly sorry for your loss. We hope that him being home helps you during the grieving process.

Our condolences,

Pet General

Michael lets the paper fall and picks up the box. The underside slides open, revealing a plastic sandwich bag filled with gray powder... "Ashes, they're his ashes."

This is what's left of him...

He sinks into a chair and runs his thumb over the bag, as if kneading Zylo's fur. Old and new anger smolder in his skull, but it's dowsed by the reminder of loss in his hand. *He deserves more than a plastic bag... He didn't deserve to be murdered, either.*

His throat hitches, and he sniffles.

"Fuck, I miss you, buddy. So damn much."

But he can't dwell too long or he'll miss the bus. Slightly more invigorated, Zylo now fresh in the forefront of his mind, he stands, placing the bag back into the box and sealing it. To keep it safe, he puts it on the counter by the coffeepot. Moves it toward the corner, to the pot, to the back wall, to the corner again... *Dammit, don't start this right now! I have to get to the bus.* An inch left, right, down, left, right...

Good. *I'll get a nice urn for him, put him somewhere in the house that I'll always see. Maybe the bedroom, once I go in there; or the living room, where he spent hours sleeping on the couch, or in here, where he'd always do that little dance when he came inside, excited for his treats*—Michael shakes his head. Doesn't want to reminisce anymore.

On the way out, he grabs the manilla folder left on the steps.

He stares out the snow-flecked window as Carlysle City gives way to a vast slate sky over open, harvested farmland. Billboards appear every few miles, shouting to purchase fireworks, to call a number to find out if you're going to Hell, to take Exit 86 to dine at a rustic-themed all-you-can-eat buffet.

It's been years since Michael's been to Cherry Brooke. The last time, he thinks, was maybe a year after Kayla and him lived in his old house. They were celebrating something important—*maybe Kayla got a promotion?*—and went to an expensive Italian restaurant downtown, then went to the Eldritch Theatre across town to watch *Sweeney Todd*. Afterward, they found a hole-in-the-wall ice cream shop offering a variety of unusual flavors, like barbecue and horseradish, and to top off the night, rode the Quercus Incline to the peak of the cliff side. They nestled together, looking at the city lights reflected on the tranquil black Refleski Lake, matching the stars overhead.

It was one of the nicest times they ever had together. That part of his life with her was great, too. He was writing, books were selling, his publisher hadn't gone defunct, his mental health had been manageable and barely affected their relationship; Zylo was back home, waiting for their late-night return. Michael loves Aaron, but he longs for the days when he and Kayla were free to do whatever they wanted, whenever. But, now... "I have neither of them, so what's freedom matter anyway?"

Farmland and hillsides give way to freeways and exits, a skyline replacing the woodsy horizon. Skyscrapers jut toward the heavens. Michael reclines, closing his eyes for the first time in what feels like days. He mentally prepares himself for the bombardment of senses once he leaves the bus. People. Noise. Smells. Cars. A cacophony of jarring, blaring racket. It'll be even worse than normal since it's December, and every shop known to man will be playing X-Mas music. *Just get to the library. No stopping. Grab food and drink somewhere close—a coffee shop or something. Library might have one, some do.*

He opens his eyes as they enter Cherry Brooke, taking a wide turn onto an elevated road. To the west, rows of empty office complexes available for sale contrast sharply with the woods behind them, and to the east, the sea of rooftops, churches, and other washed-out buildings dissected by congested streets and sidewalks. The bus descends into the thick of the city.

Michael takes out a scrap of paper with directions to the library. Craning his neck, he discovers he's on 36th Street. Checks the paper. *Get off at Thirty-Ninth, go straight, then—*

The bus slows, and he focuses on the street signs as they pass. Bundled people skitter and slide from one shoveled sidewalk to another, weave between vehicles, breathe into their gloved hands. Some huddle against street poles, smoking cigarettes or drinking coffee from Styrofoam cups.

"Thirty-Seventh...

"Thirty-Eighth..."

He grabs the overhead wire.

"Thirty-Ninth."

He pulls, an electronic bell dings, and the bus comes to a stop. Michael gives a fast wave to the driver as he steps out onto the ashy street. Wind immediately smacks him, throwing his hair back, stinging his skin. Keeping his head down, he rushes down 39th Street. People pass by, unnoticing or uncaring, but others shoulder him, nearly knocking him onto his ass. White tufts come out from his open mouth, and the hand holding the directions cold-burns terribly.

Reaches the corner of 39th and 40th. Take a... "Does that say left?" *Shit, my handwriting's awful. Looks like left. Sure, fine.*

Another bout of gale cuts through him. His runny nose is on fire, and mucus streams into his mouth. The sidewalk becomes less busy, less noisy. Wiping his lips on his sleeve, he reaches the end of 40th and turns onto 41st. *No one's* around, like he's in a video game and walked into an unloaded section of the map. The snowfall strengthens. Stoic buildings possess numberless dark windows void of life, or are those shadows behind the dark glass? Salt-stained parked cars sit along the side of the road without passengers, frosted over. Snow heaps over the bottoms of street lamps.

How is it so quiet here? I'm in the city. It doesn't even get like this back home.

The directions say left again, but the farther he goes, the more derelict it becomes. Fewer cars. Fewer working lights. More alleyways, weirdly vacant of litter and dumpsters. The afternoon sky darkens as though it's on the cusp of evening. *It can't be later than two.* Snowdrift kicks into his face, and the temperature plummets.

Where the hell am I? He can't feel his nose anymore, nor his cheeks. Snot crusts his upper lip. At the end of the block, the whipping paper with his directions says, *right then straight.* Soon the white piles are replaced by trash bags, a couple torn, spewing forth a featureless gray ooze over the unshoveled sidewalk. There aren't any more street signs, and what ones there are stare back blankly. The faded buildings intrude upon Michael's space, pressing up against him, alleys narrowing until no person could go through them. It feels like they're getting shorter, bowing over, gazing down on the man lost in the concrete labyrinth.

"I gotta get the fuck outta here."

There's a shop around the bend unlike the shuttered places he's passed. The dimly lit window in its wooden door seems welcoming, a beacon. Above it, a swinging, creaking sign says *Olaf's Ossuary.*

What's an ossuary?

Does it matter? My hands and feet are freezing, it feels like they're on fire.

He checks his directions, uncertain if he had written them down correctly to begin with or if his handwriting really is the root of the problem.

Just go in and ask the guy for help.

The heat inside is stifling compared to outside, like walking into a sauna. He removes his hands from his pockets and unzips his jacket. Inlaid shelving crammed with books and knickknacks line the hall leading into the showroom. In the center stands a large round table with dozens of old books stacked atop. A black chandelier hangs over it, exuding a candlelight glow. More shelving along the walls, housing even *more* dusty tomes and antiques.

"Hello?" Michael calls. "Anyone here?"

"Coming, coming," someone says from behind a curtain in the back. A moment later, a thin, tall, bald man slides out through it. "Greetings, I'm Olaf and welcome to my ossuary. How can I assist you?" He comes closer, and Michael catches himself before shrinking back.

His waxy skin's like drying mud, and his beady, black eyes seem to twinkle.

"Sir?"

"Sorry," Michael spurts. "Do you know how to get to the library? I think I got lost."

"More common than you think." He comes around the table. Runs his long hand down the sleeve of his black suit, brushing away dust. "It's easy to get lost in such a behemoth."

"Yeah... So, the library?"

"If you don't mind me asking," he says, ignoring the question. "What are you looking for in the library?"

Michael takes in the store. *He has all these books. He might have what I'm looking for here. Could save myself time, really.*

"I'm looking for information about this old religious group, more really a cult, the Followers of Fenrir."

"The *Følgere*? Haven't heard of them in quite some time, surprised they're still relevant." He scratches the underside of his pointed chin. "Why have they caught your interest?"

Michael knows he'll sound crazy, but says it anyway: "I think they killed my dog."

"Oh, that's horrendous, utterly horrible. Even after so many years, I can't fathom such heathens still exist. I'm so sorry for your loss." His eyes gloss over. "I once had a partner, such a beloved creature, who used to scurry around this very shop."

"What happened to them?"

"Old age, unfortunately." He wipes his eyes. "Enough about my woes. I feel your reasoning is very justified to seek out the *Følgere*."

"So you know about them?"

"Absolutely, I do. You don't manage an antique shop for this long and not learn a bit about old sects." Olaf spins and goes back through the curtain. "I may have what you're looking for," he shouts, "and something else that might interest you."

Michael meanders, listening to Olaf move things elsewhere. A framed oil painting hangs on the far wall of an elegant, pale woman with brown hair streaming down her shoulders. Nearby, a display case holds diamond rings, ruby and sapphire necklaces, wristbands and anklets encrusted with emeralds and topazes. If it weren't for the dust, Michael imagines they'd sparkle. Another shelf houses ornate silver boxes and jewelry chests, golden tiaras and ring holders.

"Ah, here we are," Olaf says, and Michael faces him. He brushes aside a stack on the table and sets three books down. "I don't believe even the library has these."

Thin and hardback with dull-colored spines. "I can't read the titles," he says, noticing they're in a foreign language.

Olaf grins, revealing narrow, yellowed teeth. "That's what's special with these." He opens one, holding it to Michael. "They're misprints." There's English on the inside, except for the title, and there's no copyright section.

"How could they misprint only the cover?"

Olaf shrugs. "I don't know, perhaps the manuscripts were removed from their original housing and rebound in these, or merely could've been the printer's mistake. Binding was very different back then—no automations, no machines, all hand-done. I'm sure mishaps occurred all the time, like you getting lost."

Yeah, but—

"Would you be interested in buying them?"

He flips through the books. They look like what he's searching for, but he didn't plan on buying anything. He hasn't checked his bank account lately, but he's sure he can't afford anything beyond bus fare and the inevitable vet bill he'll receive.

"They're nice, but I don't think I have the money," he says, setting them down. "I'll just have to take my chances at the library—"

"Nonsense! How much can you afford?"

"I'm sorry but I don't have—"

"Please, answer the question." Olaf's eyes expand. "I may be able to let them go for a lower price."

"How come?"

"Verily, I feel terrible about your dog, and if these will help you in your pursuit, then I want you to have them. Moreover, they will simply molder here if you don't take them. Hardly any living soul today knows about the Followers, nor truly cares."

Michael takes out his wallet and counts the few bills, keeping a couple dollars for the bus. "I can only do twenty," he offers meekly.

"Deal." Olaf plucks the cash from his grasp.

Being more than ready to leave, he still says: "What about that other thing you mentioned?

"Oh, yes..." Olaf draws a purple velvet satchel from his jacket. "I received this in a trade a long time ago from a trickster who attempted to convince me into assisting him in the murder of his nephew, or was it his step-nephew...?"

What did he say? I must've misheard. "What happened?"

"I don't know. He left the shop with what he wanted and I haven't heard of him since." Olaf shakes his head, nearing Michael. "His pursuit doesn't matter, but this may matter to you."

Undoing the black drawstring, Michael peers in.

Something slimy lies within, a grotesque ribbon or some fucked-up collar...

Are those actual cat paws, wrapped in... is that hair? Wait, are those roots or more hair? Definitely not hair. And, is that red-and-purple rope around them? What the hell are those small reddish-pink things? God, it reeks like a bunch of birds.

Who the hell made this, and why would anyone want it?

"Don't let first impressions fool you, this item is extremely rare— only one of its kind."

Michael steps back, the awful aroma stuck in his nose. "I don't think I'll need it, thank you, though."

He closes in on Michael. "It's always good to be prepared for all potential outcomes."

Michael takes another step back. "I don't want it."

"You may."

Jesus, leave me alone. "No."

The space is crossed once more, Olaf towering over him, eclipsing the chandelier's light. Michael's back presses against the wall. *"Yes."*

Michael sweats; suddenly the room is scorching. His stomach knots. "I don't have the money, even if I wanted it."

"Money is not what I want in this bargain."

He swallows what little saliva is in his mouth. "Then, what do you want?"

"If this item is beneficial to you, I'd like a souvenir from the ordeal."

A souvenir, from what? "And if I don't use it?"

"Simply return it, or if you prefer, you can give me your address and I'll retrieve it from you at a later point in time."

"That's it?"

"That's it," Olaf says, grinning, his sallow cheeks dimpling.

"Fine, then. Just give me a pen or something."

Olaf smoothly recedes from Michael's proximity, tying the satchel and setting it atop the books. "Wonderful." A slip of paper and pen is withdrawn from one of his pockets, and he holds them out to him.

Michael cautiously takes them and quickly writes his address. Instantly regrets not putting a fake address. Olaf gathers them with his large hand, the other pushing the stack toward him. "Now that's settled, I hope you find what you're looking for, but alas, I encourage you to leave soon. The ossuary's closing shortly, and the city's quite treacherous to navigate in the night."

"Night?"

"Yes, the sun set a little while ago."

How is it night? I got off the bus at one. He can't be right.

"Sir, I insist you be on your way," Olaf says, gaze boring into him.

Unease swells inside him. "Ah... Okay, thanks." He grabs his newly bought items, and goes down the hall and out the door without looking back. Outside, the weather devours what body heat he once had. The sodium lamps illuminate the ground in yellow, sky no longer gray but black.

This can't be right. It can't have been five hours. I was in there for half an hour, tops.

He can't remember clearly, the memory of getting to the shop and being inside already hazy. Checking over his shoulder, he finds the ossuary door closed, the window dark, the sign unmoving. He debates knocking but chooses against it. The last thing he wants is to be in the same room as that fucking weirdo again.

Then it dawns on him.

"I'm going to miss the bus!"

Strangely it takes Michael less time to return to civilization than leaving it, sprinting headlong the way he believes he came. The way back has regular buildings, people out and about, cars going up and down the street—there's life when there had been none before. But he doesn't give it too much thought in his flight, reaching the bus as it begins leaving. He beats on the closed door and screams for the driver to let him in, which thankfully he does.

As soon as Michael drops into a seat, fatigue blankets him like lead. Listlessly, he stares out the window into the night. The world feels distant, like he's aboard a spaceship peering into the nothingness of space at the blue marble growing smaller by the minute. The planet's so minuscule it's impossible for him to be concerned or notice the doings of the flea-sized people infesting it.

His stomach grumbles, he picks his dry lips, and his eyes sting when he blinks. He has no desire to leave his seat, thinking he'd prefer to be a passenger forever. It's more effort than he likes to admit to hold on to the railing when the vehicle brakes abruptly. Soon, the *Welcome to Carlysle City* sign flashes by, and even sooner than he wants, he's wrenching himself to his feet, tugging on the pull cord above.

Small-town cold is the same as the city's. His shoes crunch on the sidewalk. The colored lights strung on porches and the lit candles flanking front stairs and the oversized candy cane in the lawns help him avoid patches of ice on his way home. His house comes into view, practically an abyss beside the neighbors' decorations, and a car idles outside it, exhaust billowing from its pipe. Nearing, he makes out Kayla's face in the cherry glow of the cigarette in her mouth. Aaron's in the back seat, sleeping.

What's she doing here?

When did she start smoking?

And why the hell is she smoking with him in the car?

He raps on the driver's side window, causing her to jump and curse before rolling it down. "Where the *fuck* have you been?"

"What do you—" he starts, but doesn't want to stand anymore. "Just come inside, Kayla."

The books and bag lie on the kitchen table by the computer. The house's heat is cranked up. He turns a chair toward the hall and sits, leaning on his elbows on his knees. The front door slams shut and Kayla storms into the room.

"Where's Aaron?" he says.

"Left him in the car," she says, brow furrowing.

"Why are yo—"

"Where have you been, Michael?"

He quickly sifts through his memories of the last week, two, maybe a month, but nothing out of the ordinary emerges, besides the obvious and today. "Here," he says, "or the library."

"Are you telling me you've been *home* this whole time?"

"Uh-huh..." He nods. "Whole time. Why?"

She closes her eyes, pinches the bridge of her nose, and sighs. "I've been trying to get a hold of you since yesterday! You were supposed to get Aaron off the bus today."

His stomach drops. "Today?" *What day is it? Friday? Wednesday?*

Days bleed together in his mind. Yesterday feels like last week, last week like last month, or maybe two months ago. He tries to pinpoint the date of Zylo's death or when he visited the local library to anchor himself, but can't, time meshed together into a smear of events that for all intents and purposes may as well be lost.

"Yeah, today. You get him off the bus on Wednesday, remember?"

If today's Wednesday, then...

"Get out of your damn head and listen. You weren't there and it's freezing, and you left your son to sit out on the porch and wait for me to get home." She throws out her arm as though chucking poison at him. "Three hours later! Three! In this cold! With this wind! He could barely feel his face and hands by the time I got him inside. You're fucking lucky he didn't get frostbite!"

"Why—" His tongue numb, mouth being disobedient. He licks his lips, tries again: "Why didn't you call?"

"Do you think I'm stupid? I did! Dozens of times. But you never picked up, ever. Not once."

He glances at the phone jack, the computer still plugged in. *Fuck.* "If I didn't pick up, why didn't you come to the house?"

"Holy shit." She laughs, eyes glossing over. "Are you fucking serious? You're an adult, Michael, and he's your son. I know Zylo died and all, but I shouldn't have to check up on you to make sure you're being a father when it's necessary. But again, here I am dealing with your shit."

He wants to argue, bring up her smoking in the car, or if it was this important she should've stopped by when he didn't answer, or how she wasn't concerned for him when he didn't pick up the phone—for all she knew he could've died... But he's beyond tired and no matter how many reasons he comes up with, ultimately he knows he's wrong. Absolutely wrong. *I should've been home. Not in my head. Not chasing for information, looking for clues. Not in the city. Home. Should've been there to pick up Aaron after school. Should've done this and that... But no one's doing anything about Zy—*

"Do you have anything to say or are you just going to sit there?"

"Sorry," he says, "sorry. I should've been there."

She shakes her head. "Jesus, that's it? No 'I'll make it up to you' or 'I'll try to be better,' just you're *sorry*? Are you even still taking your meds?"

That's what it was! He nods automatically, although that's another thing he's forgotten until now.

"It's fucking funny... You doing this. I was being generous to let you have visits with him alone—you know that? My parents said you were unfit, that your mental health was too bad. They pushed for supervised visits, but no, I said, 'He's Aaron's father, and he's in therapy and taking medication. He's better, he'll be okay,' and look what happens."

"It was only once." It sounds pathetic the moment the words leave him.

"Yeah, *once*, but when will it happen again? I don't know, and I can't rely on *hoping* you'll be there to get him off the bus next week, or watch him when he comes over, or show up when he needs you."

He puts his head in his hands, closes his eyes, and sighs. Michael wishes he would've stayed on the bus. *I admitted I was wrong; isn't that enough? Doesn't she understand I'm sorry? It won't happen again...* Deep down, he knows he's lying to himself. With his dog's murder unresolved, it very well *could* happen again. No matter what he has at stake, he can't quell the obsession, the drive to find the Followers, to make them pay for what they did.

His mind won't allow it.

His heart won't allow it.

He won't allow it.

"Michael!"

His eyes shoot open, he inhales sharply.

"Have you been taking your meds?"

"I said I was."

He meets her eyes. His red-rimmed with dark bags underneath. Her's pink-tinged and glossy. He knows she knows he's lying. He knows she knows that he's not in therapy. Kayla's not dumb, and even after the divorce, she can read him like a book, knows him to his very core. It's like she has a map of his actions and knows exactly where he'll end up before he does.

"You have one more chance," she flatly says. "One. No more after that, Michael. But this time, it'll be on you. You'll be the one to decide when that is. You call me when you're ready to be a *real* father."

The sound of the door slamming is her goodbye.

The jarring clap of her departure remains in his skull like the applause of an audience. Her screams overlap it, building and rising into a crescendo. Finally he gets up and drags his feet to the couch and collapses onto it. The symphony of his failures come to an abrupt halt when the unconscious curtain drops.

CHAPTER 4

He stares at his purchase in the morning light, waiting for the carafe to fill. He slept all night, but the fatigue from the day before hasn't left.

Call me when you want to be a real father echoes in his skull, followed by the door slamming. *Real father, father, father... The last time he saw his father, his mother barged into his bedroom in the middle of the night. She quietly closed the door. Waco, their chihuahua, woke up and began barking. His mom held the cordless phone to her ear as she crawled into his closet, cracking the door when she was inside.*

"He's in the house," she whispered. "He's going to kill us. Help us, please."

Stomping on the stairs shook the floor, but not as strong as his heart beating against his chest.

"Where the fuck are you, bitch?" Words steeped in booze. Even from his bedroom and through the closed door, Michael smelled beer. He closed his eyes tightly, squeezing his lips to keep from screaming. He wished he could do something to stop the familiar unavoidable situation, but the frigid terror coiled around his lungs and limbs he knew very well kept him glued to the bed.

"Please!" his mother wailed into the phone. "He's going to kill us!"

A blank space in his memory, then: *Him standing in the kitchen, carrying Waco, his mother sitting at the table. Wood shrapnel from the doorframe littered the blue-gray carpet. Across from them his father slouched, bony fists in his lap. Bleared, piercing blue eyes honed in on him and his mother. Two policemen stood on both sides of him, one holding his shoulder.*

"Sorry," one of them said, "but since he receives bills at this residence, legally he's allowed to do what he wants in his own home."

Michael held his pup tighter, the only comfort.

"How can he— What are we supposed to do, then?" his mother said. "This is our home. I'm the one paying those bills, the rent, buying groceries. He doesn't pay or do shit."

One officer took a deep breath, ran a hand over his bald scalp. "We'll make a call to the women's shelter, and you and your son can stay there for the night. In the morning, you can go to the courthouse—"

"You're letting him stay here, with all our stuff?"

Michael felt the rage radiating from her.

"You can take anything you want with you. We'll make sure he doesn't move while you do."

Knowing it was useless to argue, they gathered the essentials, except Michael also brought a book. He didn't expect to sleep anytime soon. As they left, an officer stopped him and said, "You can't bring the dog, they don't allow animals."

"But—"

"What do you want us to do with him?" his mother said.

"You can leave him here."

"Really?"

His father laughed. "Don't worry, honey, I won't hurt him."

"Fuck you, Jerry—over my dead body." His mother took a step forward, but the other officer cut her off, putting out his hand. Michael jerked away from the bald cop trying to take Waco from him. He couldn't protect his mother but he could him.

He tried to turn again but the cop with his mother grabbed him with his other hand so the bald one could rip the small pup from his arms. Michael screamed, tried to take him back, but was pushed toward his mother.

"Fucking pigs," she spat, "stealing a kid's dog. Let's go, Michael."

He resisted her pull once, but relented the second time.

Blank space, then: *Coming home to the back door still open, their belongings in every room thrown everywhere. The fridge open and unplugged, spoiling meat and milk exuding sour rot. Vulgar words toward his mother written in red marker across the mirrors and windows. None of that mattered as Michael raced through the house, then outside, calling for Waco over and over, but never finding him.*

"Shit." Michael wipes his eyes. He never knew what happened to Waco, but he liked to hope that someone nice and caring found him, took him in. "At least she made up for it."

A week after that night, he came home from high school to his mother in the living room holding a puppy. Small, with black-and-white hair and striking pale blue eyes. The pup toppled from his mother's lap onto the floor, running toward him. Michael barely had time to toss his book bag aside before the puppy jumped at his legs, yapping, already demanding his attention.

Why he named him Zylo, he can't remember exactly—a character from a video game?—but the dog seemed to like it. He was no Waco, but he knew he'd grow to love him just the same.

Michael fills his mug and sets it on the table. Feeling a little better, he takes the satchel off the books and sets it on the counter. He catches a strong whiff of bird. "Who the hell would want this, and why was he so pushy about it? What am I going to do with it?" He shakes his head, wiping his palms on his pants. "Weirdo."

Sitting in front of the computer, he grabs the thin book on top and opens it. It's a short biography of Agnarr Enevoldsen, a man who may not or may have existed in the late twelfth or early thirteenth century.

Author's Note: It's believed that the Følgere av Fenrir *(Followers of Fenrir) was founded by Agnarr Enevoldsen. However, his very existence comes into question for there are no surviving records or evidence to indicate that he existed. The only reason we know that he may not or may have lived is through folktales passed down through generations. I have interviewed many people, old and young, and used everything supported by credible evidence to be as factual as possible. Thus, please keep this in mind while reading.*

"Should I bother reading this, then?" *This is the first time I've found something connected to the Followers. It being possibly fake doesn't change much. Knowing something is better than nothing.*

He sighs. "Alright."

Agnarr Enevoldsen was born to peasants in Kaldalr, Northern Norway. His childhood isn't known, but we do know that he grew into a broad and tall teenager; however, it helped very little with a family living in poverty. One day, a traveling merchant came to Kaldalr and he saw Agnarr, and wanted to take him on as an apprentice. Agnarr refused to abandon his family. However, his parents preferred to have their bellies and pockets full instead of a son, and sold him to the merchant...

Michael flips ahead.

Many years later, the merchant and Agnarr resided at an inn in a village close to Narvik, a small town near present-day Ofotfjord Lake. Unbeknownst to them, the religious sect, Forkynner av Æsir *(Harbingers of Aesir) were already there, adorned in colorful robes of maroon and dark blue, emblazoned with the emblem of Yggdrasil done in silver on their breast.*

"I remember that name."

Agnarr was captivated by the group for potentially many reasons: their ornamented robes, a conversation about their travels, or simply because Agnarr no longer desired to be a merchant's apprentice anymore. He wanted to speak to them, but the merchant kept him on a short leash. Thus, Agnarr waited until the merchant became inebriated like he was wont to do, and greeted the group...

"Uh-huh..."
Agnarr abandoned the merchant, likely stealing food, ale, coins, and

a horse from him, and joined the Forkynner av Æsir. *The sect traveled to various places in the country, preaching about the Old Gods (Norse gods). There was war brewing between Norway and Scotland, and many people were worried. The* Forkynner *proclaimed the Old Gods would offer protection from the Scottish if people believed in them, joined their cause, and...*

Michael comes to the final two pages.

Agnarr departed the Forkynner *for reasons unknown. Some speculate that he no longer believed their teachings, others believe he was removed. Nonetheless, he was no longer among their tribe, however still had belief in the Old Gods. However, Agnarr subscribed to the ideals that the Old Gods shouldn't simply protect them from the forthcoming conflict, but vanquish their enemies. He didn't want to be only saved—he wanted the* Scottish *eliminated.*

Others joined his cause, and Agnarr created his own sect, the Følgere av Fenrir *(Followers of Fenrir). They believed that Fenrir's chain should be broken, so he can begin Ragnarok. He would devour their enemy, but not solely the Scottish, any enemy of the Norwegian people. Fenrir would also bestow godlike powers to the* Følgere *for their devotion...*

The group mimicked the Forkynner *by traveling across Norway and preaching. Their reasoning isn't known, but for whatever purpose, they had rested at a tavern in Hoven, a village five to seven kilometers from present-day Oslo. One evening the group were inebriated, however it was well known Agnarr took to the drink the most.*

For unknown purposes, he left the tavern and confronted someone or many people, or they confronted him. There's speculation that this person or people openly opposed Følgere's *beliefs. In all likelihood an argument occurred and violence followed.*

The following day, Agnarr Enevoldsen was found dead on the riverbank by a local fisherman. He had been disemboweled so severely it was believed it couldn't have been a man or men who did the horrendous act, but a pack of wolves known to roam the forest.

Despite Angnarr's demise, the Følgere's *mission didn't falter. They continued spreading their message throughout Norway until at least until the turn of the century. Nothing is known of them after that point in time. They had all but vanished, and the* Følgere av Fenrir *fell into obscurity.*

Michael closes the book, glances at the others on the table. *Is it even worth reading the other two?* Only one book deep and already worn out of reading. His attention span's dwindled since he stopped writing and reading regularly, back when his publisher went under. One more thing he misses from then. Back to the computer, he searches for *Agnarr Enevoldsen.*

Surprisingly, two websites appear. He expected nothing to show. The first offers a poorly scanned version of the book he just read, though now he knows the title and author: *Agnarr Enevoldsen: A Misguided and Short Life,* by Neil McCoy. No publication date, but he guesses it would've been written sometime in the early 1900s. Then he wonders why someone would bother writing a biography about Agnarr at all, or how anyone knew enough about him to do so. He hadn't accomplished much in his life, from what he read, and unlike many mythological heroes, he wasn't a great soldier, wasn't a mighty king or cruel god, didn't do anything notable besides founding an obscure cult. Hell, it was very likely he never existed, either.

Biographies are written about so many different people all the time—this isn't much different.

He shrugs, closes out the window, and clicks on the other website. The screen flashes white, black, then static, like a TV without an input, with horizontal strobing lines. The URL bar rapidly transforms from English into weird letters and characters, then into a different URL, then another... Stops.

"Wllfwrld," he says. It's a blank, black screen with a text box in the middle, PASSWORD written within.

"Uh..." He takes a shot in the dark, typing: *Fenrir.*

Denied.

Then: *Agnarr.*

Denied.

Norse, Norway, Runes, Viking...

Denied, denied, denied, denied.

It has to be something related to Agnarr, he feels, because why else would it come up when he searched his name? And what the hell could it be otherwise? Growing frustrated, he reopens the book to the beginning. One hand pinning it open, he pecks the keyboard with the other:

Kaldalr.

Denied.

"What about..." *Enevoldsen.*

Denied.

"Mother—" Michael's seethes.

From the last page, he tries: *Hoven.*

Approved.

The black screen dissipates into pixelated dust, revealing a message board with a gray background and light blue text. The contrast of colors is difficult to look at directly. There's a single thread, titled *The Well* posted by user ITRUEND. It's locked from any new comments being made, but he can click into it. Inside, a video is embedded into the post. Michael's thankful, threadbare already from reading this morning.

He presses play.

A person wearing a dark gray wolf mask with their hood up, illuminated by the blue light of seemingly their computer, takes up the whole shot. Interlaced, weaving black lines run up the jaw, splintering down the snout and ascending between the sickly yellow eyes, past the pointed ears, meeting in the center, then down to the forehead to create the *Svulek.* Small parts of the eyes are cut out, revealing human, green eyes.

"*The time has come,*" ITRUEND says, voice deep, distorted. "*Yggdrasil has been dug from the same soil He was slain on years ago, its roots nourished by the Basins around the world with our offerings.*

"*He could not believe what we would do in only the last decade. We would be praised. He would celebrate us! We should be proud of what we have done and what we will do. The gods will look at us in awe once Ragnarok happens.*

"*Unfortunately, not all Followers can witness Yggdrasil, but know we are grateful to everyone who harvested. Together we have more than enough to feed to the Devourer of Worlds. Without you, we would not be able to do what must be done.*

"*Followers, the time is near—have your candles ready to be lit, for the Winter Solstice will be the world's darkest day.*"

The video ends. There's nothing else to it, no URLs or text listed in the post. "'Winter Solstice will be the world's darkest day'?"

They're going to try to summon Fenrir then.

"'...from which he was tragically slain.' Do they mean Hoven, where Agnarr died?"

That's insane. Impossible. Gods don't exist.

"But it makes sense: the dog killings, the books, the history; Fenrir, the runes, the mountain symbol. Everything adds up to these assholes wanting to summon him so he can eat the world."

They killed him and however many other dogs for this absolute bullshit.

Uncertainty, anger, and confusion swirls in his mind as adrenaline floods him. He can't sit anymore, so he paces around the kitchen. Every time he passes the urn, he adjusts it.

Left, right.

He knows he shouldn't allow himself to succumb to a compulsion, but anything to keep him from spiraling more is better than nothing.

Forward, back.

Trains barrel over his temples. Ice slides down the base of his skull, trickling over his spine.

"If that's true, what am I supposed to do about it?"

He's finally reached his goal. He knows who the killers are and their reasoning behind it. He could possibly stop them and avenge his pup. But should he be the one to do it? Is Zylo a good enough reason to pursue a cult into the unknown, potentially putting himself in danger? They're dog murderers. Animal killers. He couldn't fathom someone doing that, let alone what they'd do to a person. Or is this his obsessiveness getting the better of him like many times before, fixated on something he has no business being a part of? Or is this what he actually wants, what he's meant to do?

"Maybe I should call the police, let them handle it."

I've said that a dozen times now, what don't I get? They aren't going to do anything.

"True, plus they'd take all the proof I have and shove it in a cabinet somewhere to never be seen again."

I also have no clue who the cultists are specifically, or the one who did *kill him. From the video, there's apparently several of these little groups, but the main one is in Norway. I'm not that much of an idiot to think that Carlysle City Police will go out of their way to talk to whoever's there.*

His shaking hands move the urn across the counter.

Forward, back.

Perspiration covers Michael. Did he turn the heat down after last night? His thoughts become a blur, too fast to decipher before another takes its place.

Stay or go.

Give up or continue.

Let his death mean nothing, or make it worth something.

He closes his eyes and bites his bottom lip, wanting to scream. To close off every part of himself and dwindle into nothing. To explode and release all the fucking pressure building inside him. To exist but not, drift in a void between worlds.

"I don't know what the fuck to do!"

Right, left.

Forward—

"There!"

He releases the urn and falls back into the kitchen chair. His shirt sticks to his heaving chest. He laughs, frowns.

It has to be me. I don't want it to be.

In the bathroom, he takes in his reflection in the mirror. *Have I always looked like shit? Jesus, the bags under my eyes are deep purple. It looks like I lost some weight, too, pretty gaunt. And I'm so greasy.* His black shirt has a white stain from somewhere, and when did he last wash these pants? *It's like I haven't slept or eaten in weeks.* He pulls back his hair, leaning over the sink. *Grays coming in, too. Great. I'm surprised Kayla didn't mention something.*

"Gotta take my medicine." It feels strange saying it, words he hasn't spoken in God knows how long. He takes the bottle from the medicine cabinet behind the mirror. Feels stranger holding it. Kayla had been right, like always. He *needs* these to avoid any pitfalls, especially going forward. There's no way he'll be able to fully function when—not *if*—his mind unfurls, his compulsions taking over his body. His thoughts require some semblance of clarity if he's to travel overseas, not to mention the anxiety that'll inevitably overwhelm him must be quelled to some degree. He shakes the bottle before opening it as though it may be empty.

After shaking two into his hand, he tosses them into his mouth, the familiar chalky taste on his tongue, and uses the tap to wash them down. Since he's been off them for a while they'll work quicker, maybe, and doubling up will get him better faster, hopefully. Setting the capped bottle on the counter, he undresses away from the mirror—no desire to see how shriveled he has become—and gets into the shower.

In the kitchen, the meds rattle in his pocket while he makes a sandwich and coffee, then does the dishes he had left out before. Snowflakes passing by the kitchen window twinkles in the darkness outside.

Michael decided in the shower that he'll have to go after them, no matter how terrified it makes him just thinking about it. He doesn't know what will happen when he meets the Followers, what he will say, what he will do, but it's better than doing nothing. They killed his fucking dog, and they at least deserve to hear the damage they brought to his life. It could be his mental illness, could be the pills, could be a placebo, could be stubbornness, could be anything, but he doesn't care —it's happening, regardless of the reason.

The travel agency website slowly loads on the computer. He sets his plate and cup down, leaning toward the monitor.

"Really need to upgrade to DSL at some point."

It finally loads. All he needs is the number at the bottom. He plugs in the phone, dials. It's a quick conversation with a lady from InterTravels. He books a flight to Olso, Norway from Cherry Brooke, PA for December 18, with a layover in Alta. He uses his credit card to pay, knowing he won't be able to pay it off anytime soon unless he begins writing again. *But fuck it.*

After hanging up, he calls Kayla.

"Hey—"

"What do you want, Michael?"

"I want to see Aaron tomorrow."

Silence.

"Are you taking your meds?"

"Yup." He pads his pocket. "Never stopped."

"Why tomorrow?"

"I'm leaving town for a bit. Not sure when I'll be back."

"Leaving *town*?"

He grits his teeth, not wanting to argue. "I have something to do— Can I just see him? I'll get him off the bus after school, take him to the park, then have dinner."

"Should I ask why you're leaving or where you're going?"

"Better if you didn't. So can I see him or what? You told me to call when I wanted to be a father. Here I am."

More silence.

"Okay, just the park and dinner, then he has to come home right after, even if it's the weekend."

"Great," he says, smiling. "Thank you, Kayla."

"You're welcome," she says, "but you better be there when he gets off that bus next time, Michael. I've given you many chances, but I'm not doing that with Aaron. I won't let you hurt him again."

He promises he won't, and they say their goodbyes.

Throughout the night Michaels reads online as much about Norway as he can: roads, towns, bus routes, and so on. Taking notes all the while, creating a loose plan for when he arrives in Oslo. He figures the most obvious place where the Followers are meeting is in Hoven; second likely place is Kaldalr. Both fifteen or so miles apart, but he has only a day to figure out which. From a website barely translated into English, he deciphers that a public bus regularly runs from Oslo past Hoven, then through the countryside close to Kaldalr, which works out well. He can catch the earliest one in the morning.

How will I know who they are? What will they look like? Will they be wearing anything out of the ordinary? How can someone tell if someone's in a cult, besides the guy from the video with a mask?

"Too late for that now." He'll deal with it when it comes.

The meds haven't been in him long enough to prevent the uncertainty looming over him. Michael hates the unexpected, hates change, and the upheaval of this life when Zylo's passing is like being thrown into the ocean without a life jacket. His mind and body tell him to stop, to return to what he knows, the familiar. Keep everything the same, because change is scary, unknown, *wrong*.

Somewhere in the recesses of his skull, he knows it hasn't been as terrible as his anxieties want him to believe.

I'm alive, ain't I?

Something catastrophic happened and I'm still standing. My brain hasn't melted. My eyes haven't exploded. Blood hasn't erupted from my pores. I'm worse for wear, but the same as I was before. The world hasn't swallowed me.

Not yet, anyway.

Melancholy trickles into the house, casting periwinkle. Michael finishes his rough plan by the time the sun rises. He yawns, and looks at the clock. Six thirty a.m. Aaron gets off the bus around two p.m., so he can get everything packed and the house put together, and take a nap before having to get him. Afterward, they can go to the store together for dinner, and he can let his son choose what they're eating. Michael hopes it's not ketchup sandwiches, one of his favorites.

He tucks Zylo's urn into the top cabinet for safe keeping, then carries his computer and printer back into the office. Puts the books and bag he got from Olaf, and clothes from the pile in his office and toiletries, in a duffle bag he found in the hallway closet.

"Meds," he says, tossing the bottle inside. "Can't forget those."

His bedroom door keeps closed. It has things he might need, but even standing before it makes his hands shake, his flesh prickle with trepidation. Zylo's squeaky toy still on his unmade bed; his own bed by the vent, vacant; an encapsulated past he dare not disturb yet. He brings the packed duffle downstairs, putting it in the living room on his way to the couch to sleep.

The last time Michael had been to the park was in the summer, soon after the divorce, with Aaron and Zylo. Now, snow covers the graffitied jungle gym, heaps at the bottom of the rusted slide, tiny piles on what swings are there. Cars blend together behind him, driving through slush. Memories of that final day begin to surface, but he pushes them down. *Today's about Aaron.*

He doesn't remember it looking this bad, but it has been years. "Sorry," he says to his son. He brushes off a picnic table to set Aaron's book bag onto it.

"About what?" he says, looking up at Michael. Snowflakes cling to his dark blue toque.

Does he not see how bad it is? I should probably keep it that way. "Nothing, so what do you want to hit first?"

"The slide—race you there!"

Aaron takes off, Michael purposefully following behind. He stops, watching his son clank up the metal stepladder to the top. Aaron sits and shoves off down the chute. He screams going down, and Michael quickly gets to the bottom before Aaron does to make sure he doesn't drop into an unnoticed icy puddle below.

The snow bursts and his son emerges from the cloud of white, smiling, laughing. Michael grabs him midair, spinning, and nearly loses balance before putting him down. "Wow, you're fast, bud."

"I can do it faster!"

Again, Aaron sprints back up the slide. True to his word, he reaches the top quicker than before. Michael goes to catch his son once more, but Aaron reaches the bottom before he can prepare. Aaron shoots out and crashes into Michael, toppling him over.

Hitting the hard earth knocks the air from his lungs, and it takes a moment to catch his breath. Aaron rolls off him, kneeling beside him. "Are you okay, Dad? I didn't mean to go *that* fast."

Michael ignores the pain in his chest, knowing there will be a bruise. Instead of replying, he laughs. It makes it hurt worse, but it also feels good, too. Laughing makes it seem like everything awful that's been happening is miles and miles away. It's as if he's finally free, some burden until now weighing on his mind, shoulders, lifted. Being engrossed in his pup's pursuit, the cult, everything that's led up to this point. The first time he hasn't been obsessing, his mind mostly clear, being in the *present*, focusing on Aaron. Though, a tinge of guilt ripples through him, like by not having him forefront in his thoughts he's somehow disrespecting him, his death.

"Dad, are you okay?" Aaron says again, shaking him. "Dad—"

Michael scoops his son into his arms, growling like a monster, and rolls over, dropping him onto the ground, leading to a full-blown snowball fight. Father and son dart around the park, hiding, throwing. Michael's hit in the face, and Aaron gets one in the back of the head. The slate sky darkens. The streetlamp by the picnic tables turns on. Headlights pass by. Before they know it, they're soaked, and hungry.

Michael hunches over, breathing labored. Sweat or water or both makes his hair stick to his forehead. "Alright, you win, let's go get dinner."

Aaron wipes his face with the back of his glove. "What are we getting?"

"Whatever you want."

"Really?" he shouts.

"Yup, let's go."

Luckily, Aaron's choice is cheap and takes little time to make: spaghetti with meat sauce and buttered Italian bread. He comes into the kitchen, his auburn hair sticking up every which way, and says, "Is it done?"

Michael pours the noodles into the strainer, billowing steam fogging the windows. The oven fan roars, while sauce bubbles in a pot on a burner. "Almost, bud."

He dumps the spaghetti into a large metal bowl, switches off the stove and fan, and sets everything onto the table on folded rags. The sliced Italian bread and butter are almost forgotten, but join the fray.

Before he has the chance to sit, Aaron's already reaching over his plate for the tongs in the spaghetti.

"Whoa!" Michael says, taking the tongs. "Let me get that for you."

Aaron sits back, and his father fixes a plate for the both of them. It's quiet as they focus on eating. He steals glances at Aaron. The warmth of cooking after being outside, the smell of the food, the sound of him slurping and splashing sauce on his cheeks... Michael yearns to remain here, stuck in this moment, because he knows once he leaves, he isn't sure when he'll see him again. *Who knows what will happen? Who knows how everything will turn out? I could end up like Zylo.*

And even though speaking would ruin it, he still says, "So... I'm going away for a bit."

"Where you going?"

"Just away, to see someone about Zylo."

"Are you seeing the police?" Aaron looks up from his plate. "Has he been a good police dog?"

"Not exactly, but something like that, and he's been the best police dog they've ever seen."

"I know he's helping to catch bad guys... But I wish I could see him. I miss him a lot."

"Me too."

They fall back into quiet, returning to their meals. Aaron finishes his plate, wipes his mouth with his hand, smearing red sauce across his cheek. "Can I have more?"

Michael laughs, the mood instantly lighter. "You can have as much as you like, but after you clean your face off."

Around seven, Kayla knocks on the front door. *Always punctual.* He carefully slides out from under Aaron's head on his lap on the living room couch, and opens the door.

"Welcome back," he whispers.

"How was it?"

"Good. Played at the park, ate, and watched a little TV." He softly closes the door.

"Where's he at?"

He nods to the living room. They walk in together, and look over the back of the couch. Aaron's on his side, asleep. An urge flashes over Michael to put his arm around Kayla, or grab her hand that's close to his; he'd love to be together, to be a family once more, to slip back into a part of life he remembers fondly.

If it was different, if their present wasn't built on a broken past, he'd carry Aaron up to his room—replacing the office—and tuck him into his bed. He'd tiptoe downstairs, and Kayla and him would cuddle on the couch, watching whatever TV show until late. They'd shut off the lights downstairs, and go upstairs into their bedroom. Both would dress for bed and lay under the comforter. They'd fall into their natural positions of him being the big spoon, her the little. He'd hold her close until the warmth of the blankets and her body lulled him to sleep.

Michael keeps his hand to his side.

That'll never happen again. It shouldn't. She's moved on, and to try to rekindle our marriage would cause more problems for her. She has enough shit to deal with, and my stuff doesn't need to be added to the pile.

"So you two should be going," he says. "I don't want to interrupt his sleep too much."

She moves around the sofa and lifts him up, carrying him to the entry. "Can you grab his jacket?"

He runs back to the kitchen, snatches it from the chair, and brings it back, blanketing Aaron with it. Surprisingly, his son stays asleep.

"Will you be back before Christmas, or should I say Santa's presents are going to be late this year?" she says around Aaron's head on her shoulder.

He shrugs. "I'm going to try, but if I'm not, I'll make it up to him."

They look at one another. "Be careful, Michael, with whatever you're doing."

"I will. No worries."

He watches her walk to the already running car and buckle Aaron into the back seat. She waves, giving a quick smile before getting in, and he closes the door before the car leaves.

Michael sips from a Styrofoam cup in a chair in the airport terminal. When he booked the flight he hadn't taken into consideration getting *to* the airport. The town's buses stopped running at eleven p.m., so he had to hurry to catch one. What he also didn't anticipate was that the bus's heating would be broken. He arrived four hours early for his flight and barely felt his extremities.

He beelined to the person at the help desk who pointed him in the right direction, then went through security. Michael was sort of glad he was this early. He had no need to rush, though it felt like he did. After being cleared by TSA, he grabbed a lukewarm coffee from a machine and found an empty seat.

The heat from the drink blooms in his chest. His knee bobs, and he runs a hand through his hair. A blonde flight attendant comes out from a backroom, goes to the podium by his terminal, and switches on the light above the doorway. She taps on the microphone, and speaks into it: "Flight 132 boarding for Alta, Norway. Flight 132 boarding for Alta, Norway."

He gulps the rest of his coffee, grimacing from the dregs, and tosses the empty cup into a waste bin as he walks to the podium. He hands the woman his ticket.

She scans it, and gives it back. "You're all set. Have a safe flight."

"Thanks."

He takes the ticket and moves down the narrow hall, where he passes by another flight attendant as he steps into the plane. Michael finds his economy seat by the window in the back row. Not many people board after him. A man wearing a fedora huffs when he sits across the aisle. Two women in matching large overcoats plop down a couple rows up. A mother and daughter occupy the two by the bathroom.

Michael hears the thunk of the door closing and the attendant stands in the aisle. Intently Michael listens to instructions about flying and what he ought to do in an emergency. When she finishes he peers out the window as the runway recedes from the plane. His heart lodges in his throat when they take flight, hands gripping the armrests when turbulence kicks in, and when it's over he releases the faux leather.

The world below is dark, save for pinpricks of city light. It's oddly calming, drifting in the nothingness.

Like being in space staring at stars.

CHAPTER 5

It was a feverish blur getting from the plane in Alta to the one going to Oslo, but he managed and finally arrived at the Gardermoen Airport in Oslo. Jet-lagged, Michael didn't care about the sights, the people, anything. It might've been day or might've been night, he wasn't sure. Vaguely he noticed holiday decorations plastering the walls and windows, and faint, cheery jingles playing over the speakers. Outside the airport, he caught a cab, relieved it had an English-speaking driver and that he accepted USD, to the cheapest, closest hotel.

Michael struggled with an old woman at the hotel front desk who spoke broken English, but eventually she understood him and he rented a room for the night. As he walked down the beige hallway, fatigue slowly grew in him. He'd slept most of the trip yet somehow he was still beat. He found his room and once inside, he dropped his bag, heeled the door closed, and collapsed onto bed, scratchier than it looked.

He passed out anyway.

Michael takes his meds, a shower, and changes his clothes in the morning. Getting out his legal pad, he reads over his printed notes and map, glad he didn't make the same mistake twice by hand-writing anything.

"The bus to Hoven leaves at nine a.m." He checks the bedside clock. *Only eight a.m.* "Should leave soon."

What do I have to do first?

"Convert money to kroner at the front desk, get to the bus stop, take the bus to Hoven. Find somewhere to stay there, and search for the Followers."

He shakes his hands but it fails to get rid of the tingling. He takes a deep breath in, out. It feels like there's butterflies in his chest, like something crawls beneath his skin, wanting out. "I'll be fine." He paces the small room, his heart racing. The walls seem to close in, the sky outside the unopenable window darkening. "I'll be okay. Nothing dangerous will happen."

First time traveling. First time being in another country. First time doing anything like this. But no matter where I am or what's happening, the overwhelming feeling is the same.

"I just need to go. It always gets better once I'm doing the thing."

He goes through his luggage for a second time, ensuring everything is there, then slowly gets his jacket on. With his bag slung over his shoulder, he double-checks his wallet before leaving.

Still too anxious, he navigates the city as though he's rushing through a war zone. Tall, pastel-colored buildings lining the street go by hardly noticed. Though, he *has* to notice how the shoveled sidewalk is far more taken care of here than home. No cracks, chunks missing, or randomly one tile raised over another, weeds sprouting from below. The paved road has no potholes in sight, and none of the street lamps are burned out.

Little by little, he realizes how much *nicer* Oslo is not only to his hometown, but to even Cherry Brooke. He anticipated it to be similar to cities in the States, because he knew nothing else. Crossing the street, he stops when a tan brick mansion looms upon a hill, a slate sky above. He's never seen a house that enormous, only on TV shows. Lights are strung across the hedges bordering the property, and a giant Christmas tree stands in the center of the snow-laden yard. Michael starts counting the windows—

Stop wasting time. You'll miss the bus.

"Right."

Coming to what he believes to be a wide alley, he finds crowds of moseying, smiling, and laughing people carrying huge shopping bags. "Not Another Blue Christmas", in Norwegian, plays from speakers mounted on the light poles, echoing. As he makes his way through, he accidentally bumps into a large man.

"Unnskyld meg," he says before Michael goes to quickly apologize.

He doesn't know what to say, and the man must notice his confusion. "Sorry," he says, patting him on the shoulder and becoming lost among the throng.

Did he apologize to me *for me bumping into* him? *No screaming, no threats. What is this place? Heaven?*

Onward and beyond the alley, gradually his stress melts away and he comes to a shopping district where every storefront's frosted display windows are framed with white lights. Within are powdered evergreens, tinsel holly hung above, reflective gifts tied in ruby-red bows. One has a train set going around nutcrackers, stuffed bears, and other decor. Groups of people stand outside, smoking cigarettes, talking, drinking something warm, while many others enter and exit the shops.

It reminds him of Aaron, Kayla, possibly missing Christmas this year, and all the holidays since the divorce. He always tried to give Aaron a good X-Mas with plenty of gifts, his favorite sugar cookies with the red and green sprinkles, watched any movie or TV show of his choosing, and sometimes let him open a present the night before.

Nevertheless no matter the amount of effort or money he put in, it always felt hollow, something missing when it was only the two of them and Zylo. He guessed it was because the holidays were usually family oriented, and without a partner completing the picture, the emptiness wouldn't leave... And now, without his dog, an even greater void will form, another black hole devouring what little happiness they may have together.

Stop thinking about it.

Past the shops, he takes a left and crosses a salted street. Through an alleyway running between a gray stone church and some type of factory, he comes out by the bus stop. Glass walls and roof enclose a metal bench, where a woman wearing a jacket and scarf sits. He sighs as he walks to it, standing idly.

The red bus doesn't appear around the corner for another half an hour. He lets the woman on first, and pays the toll and takes a seat by the door. No one else gets on, the door closes, and the bus moves on. Out the foggy window, flakes begin to fall. They pass a giant, square redbrick building, drive along the sea where seagulls fly overhead in spite of the weather; there's a white, slanted building with somehow more windows than the mansion he saw before, and on a hill, he recalls from the internet, is the Royal Palace with its yellow-painted walls and green statue of a man riding a horse out front.

Gradually, the countryside replaces the city. Wire fences and wooden posts, sometimes low stone walls, contain vast fields vanishing in the snowfall. Cattle, goats, and sheep rove most of the land, a separate section where horses mill about. Farmhouses and cottages stand by the road, smoke wisps coiling out from their chimneys. In the distance, tiny houses dot the plains. *Such a better sight than the trip to Cherry Brooke.*

After a while, the snow thickens, obscuring the glass. The conversation with Kayla flits through his mind, the ultimate question lingering: *What am I going to do if I find them?* She spoke about the autopsy, but obviously he's beyond that now. Yet still, Michael doesn't completely know. Yell at them, maybe? Call the police? Punch them in the face? Or will it be a split-second decision made at the time, where logic and reason are thrown to the wayside, letting his anger, loss, frustration, everything direct his actions? He hates being unprepared, but there's not much he can do for the unknowable. *Control what I can and let what happens, happens.*

Wind howls against the bus, rocking it. The heat's turned up. Abruptly, the bus driver says something over the speakers. Michael doesn't understand what he's saying, but he catches the word "Hoven" and he yanks the cord.

Virtually impossible to see past a few feet, Michael follows the paved road into what must be Hoven. The bus disappears in the white. Pavement gives way to gravel and dirt, and squat, dark wooden homes emerge from the aether. Windows glow with soft yellow light, and cobblestone chimneys exhale smoke. A few beat-up vehicles are parked alongside the houses. No one's out, and he can't blame them with the storm.

Michael looks down at his map, but the wind makes it difficult to keep it open. He brushes it off, peering closer. *The inn should be close by.* He makes it to the center of town, an intersection. *Should be this way...* Not looking both ways, he speed-walks across. He can't see anything anyway, so the likelihood of being hit by a car is the same as if he had checked. A one-story wooden building looms ahead, an ebbing warm light filling the small windows in the front door. Burned into the wood above reads: *Hundehus. Whatever that means.* The door creaks open. As soon as he's inside, the heat of the room engulfs him, like being embraced by a giant. The door closes behind him.

Through a short corridor, he comes to the inn proper. People sit at round tables drinking and eating while a fire blazes in a stone fireplace in the far wall. Wrought iron chandeliers hang from the high-vaulted ceiling. Utensils scraping plates and chitter-chatter fills the meaty and ale-scented aromatic air. The few men and women who look at him he awkwardly nods at. At least some reciprocation. At the counter running along the opposite wall, he rings a silver bell atop.

"*Kommer, kommer,*" someone shouts from a doorway behind the counter by a corkboard, a sparse amount of keys hanging. A young woman comes out, wearing an olive hooded sweatshirt and black jeans, eyes green and blonde hair past her shoulders.

"Hello, sorry, but do you speak English?"

"Horribly!" someone shouts from behind, and others laugh.

"*Hold Kjeft!*" she shouts, Norwegian accent thick, giving the finger to the heckler, then says: "Sorry about him—I speak English well enough, I think. Name's Tabatha, what can I help you with?"

"My name's Michael, and I'm looking for a room to stay in for a night or two."

"You're lucky, we still have a few left."

"Do many people come here?"

"Not usually." She takes a key down, tossing it onto the counter. "But the festivities brings in a lot."

Festivities? Does she mean...? He swallows the lump in his throat. "Christmas?"

"I guess you could call it that, at least it is to us." She laughs. "The room will cost about five hundred kroner per night."

Their Christmas... Michael takes out his wallet, numb fingers taking him a bit to get out the money. He forgets the conversion rates, so he puts down an assortment of bills. *There's no way she's a part of the cult. She looks like someone I would've went to school with.* "Sorry," he mutters.

"Not a problem," she says, taking a couple bills, leaving the rest of them for him to take back. "American, right?"

He laughs. "That obvious?"

"Not as much as you think." Smirking, she slides the bills beneath the counter. "Your room's down the hall, by the window at the end. If you need help with anything, just ring the bell."

He says he will, and she returns to the back room.

A couple holding hands come out of one room as he enters the dimly lit yellow-brown corridor, they exchange greetings with Michael as they pass by. The doors to the rooms remind him of the flaky, dark wood paneling his parents' home had in the '80s. *This has to be real wood, not that fake crap.* Small, thin stone plaques dangle from some of the doorknobs, *No* carved into them, painted red. Michael treads softer. The din of the other guests in the commons gradually fades, and he finds his room where she said it was.

Inside's quaint with one window, a single made bed, and a nightstand with a lamp, corded phone, and digital clock. He flicks on the lights in the bathroom. Toilet, sink, shower. Turns it off and checks the nightstand drawer. Empty, not even a Bible. Outside, there's nothing-but-white to see. Michael drops his bag, sinking into the bed. Not even noon, but he's ready for sleep. Lying back, he closes his eyes.

"Just need a power nap."

Michael's stomach wakes him. It's not grumbling, but *hurting*. He sits up with a sharp inhale like coming up for air, and wipes the drowsiness from his eyes. Sun falls in through the window. He can't remember the last time he ate. *Yesterday? Two days ago?* The bedside clock says: 14:34. Quickly figures out that's: 2:34 p.m. Michael drags himself off the bed and plods into the bathroom.

Minutes later, dressed in several layers, he goes to the front counter. A few people sit around the tables now, drinking coffee or ale, reading, or staring listlessly into the dying embers in the fireplace. Tabatha leans on the counter, reading an umber-covered book. A faint sour smell comes from the room behind her, but he didn't take a shower, so he assumes it's himself. *Need to do that when I get back.*

"Hello, again," she says, putting her text aside. "Did you get any sleep?"

"Some, thank you, but do you know any restaurants around here?"

"There aren't any, but I can whip you up some food, if you like."

"If you don't mind," he says. *But what about that smell?* His gurgling stomach doesn't seem to care.

"Not for you, I don't. Pick a table and it will be out soon."

In what must be the kitchen, he hears the thunk of a cleaver hitting wood. She must be cutting meat. He looks around at the others in the room. *Are they a part of the cult, too?* He imagines what ITRUEND looks like, expecting the same from every cultist, or like in the movies: black-clad people lurking in the shadows doing their horrendous work. Pure evil. Villainous. Not regular people like Kayla, him, or anyone in his vicinity.

But the Followers *have* been around for hundreds of years, and even if their traditions were passed down generation after generation, they'd have to adapt with modern times in some way to blend in or they'd get nowhere fast. So he supposes that maybe some of them *could* be among their ranks.

Tabatha comes out holding two full plates and big mugs. She sets one of each in front of him, the other put before a vacant chair. Two large pieces of white, buttered bread flanking thin slices of meat with olives, cucumber, and an egg in the middle. The mug's filled with black coffee.

"Looks great," he says, looking from the food to her. He tries picturing her murdering an animal, scooping out organs, scarring the insides with—

"Do you mind if I join you? I forgot to ask, sorry."

"Oh!" he says, heat rushing to his face, then a second later: "Sure, absolutely."

She sits next to him. *Is she just being nice or is she flirting?* He assumes the former, because to assume the latter could end badly. He hasn't dated anyone since Kayla, and before her, he was in high school. It isn't that he has no interest in dating, but that no one seems to have shown interest in dating *him.* His heart continues to flutter a little. *Not in school anymore but I still feel the same as I did.* Instead of talking, he starts on his food.

"Do you have any plans today?" Tabatha says, eating a piece of toast.

He shrugs, splitting the egg yolk, spilling over the meat. *What sort of meat is this? Tastes like lamb or beef. It's good either way.* "Besides food, honestly no. Is there anything I *should* do around here?"

"No, not really." She laughs. "Hoven's not a normal village, it's more like a resort. People only come here once in a while."

"For the holiday?"

She nods, sipping her coffee. "Sometimes they gather for other things, but not often or always here."

His stomach rolls, appetite dissolving. The question presses against his lips, unsure if he should ask or not, but how else will he know he's in the right place? "Which holiday is it, if it's not Christmas?"

"It's like a celebration of better times to come, sort of like New Year, but it's not always a yearly tradition, if that makes sense." She crosses her fork and knife on her empty plate. "How are you enjoying the food? Did I cook good?"

He glances at his half-eaten plate, but he's no longer hungry. "You're a great cook. Way better than me." He laughs while guilt ebbs over him about not finishing his meal. She made it specifically for him, since no one else in the room is eating or seems to have eaten recently. Despite the bitterness of the coffee, he finishes it. "I'm not a big eater," he quickly adds.

"*Takk.* Since you do not have plans, would you mind if I showed you around the town? It will not be a long trip."

Really, she wants me? Sweat gathers under his arms. Her potential association with the Followers ebbs in his mind. "I don't mind at all."

Gathering their dishware, she takes them into the back, returning a moment later wearing a winter jacket. She waves him on, and he takes the cue to follow her outside.

The storm's let up, sky blue and cloudy just enough to make the sun not blinding. The short houses skirting the roads, covered in ankle-deep snow, are cozier-looking than he initially thought. Eerily similar, too. Dark wood with old shingles and stone chimneys, narrow windows, a square door with a paned peephole. It's exactly what he pictures when he thinks of the word *cottage*. A couple older people trudge along, a few middle-aged folk shovel their paths to their doors. Some cars idle, exhaust billowing.

Meandering, he peeks into a house. One level, it seems, with a hall leading farther back, and the living room encompasses most of the area. An evergreen tree topped with a white nine-pointed star stands next to an old river stone fireplace. Small rocks with painted runes in red hang on twine over the mantel. A quilt has been thrown over the back of a rocking chair sitting on the woven carpet on the hardwood, and a variety of pots sit on the stove in the kitchenette in the rear. *Are these people Amish?* There's no electronics, no phones, not even TVs far as he can tell. It's only one house, but he suspects most are like this since they all look the same. It's as though he's stepped back in time.

"The Hundehus has the only generator," she says, noticing his confusion. "Like I said, Hoven's not normal. I live the most here while others visit to get away from the ruckus of the world, celebrating a better future."

"Why do you live here if no one else does?"

"I own the inn, Hundehus is my last name. It was my grandmother's before she passed away. She was closer to my mother than my own mother."

"Sorry for your loss," he says. "What about your grandpa?"

She laughs, fog coming out of her mouth. "Now *he's* closer to a stranger than a relative. Same for my father, too."

Michael almost apologizes again, but doesn't. He's aware that some-times doing it too much makes it sound like he actually doesn't care, that he's just saying it to say it. Meaning lost. Moreover, the temptation to ask if she has any other family rises but is quelled. *God only knows if she lost them, too. I'd really feel stupid then.* So he keeps quiet.

More people come out to shovel, sprinkle salt on walkways, work on removing snow around their vehicles if they have one. *Does a plow come out here?* Then he notices there's no telephone poles, nor wires running from house to house. *I guess she is right. Everything here is temporary.*

"Do you have any family back home?" Tabatha shoves her gloved hands into her blue jacket.

"Aaron, my son, he's six, and until recently, I had a dog, Zylo, that I considered family."

"Oh no, that is awful. What happened to him?"

If she's a part of the cult, she wouldn't ask that, right? She'd know what happened, unless she's lying. And how much should I say? Should I lie, because she'd know if I was, too? Michael opens his mouth, closes it, then: "He was in an accident, a hit-and-run."

He faces her, watching her in an attempt to discern if she's lying. "Did the police find who did it?"

She seems normal. He scoffs. "I wish, but no. They're still out there, whoever did it."

"I hope they find them soon. I hate when animals die without purpose, like those people who hunt just for sport. It is sickening."

He nods, as they take a corner. A stout old man waves to Tabatha, who waves back. Michael does, too. *Why'd I do that? I don't know him.* The farther they go, the sparser the houses become. Swathes of white fields replace them, footprints leading toward a powdered spruce forest in the distance. Wind kicks up and they turn in time to avoid being hit in the face with snowdrift.

Soon, they come to the end of the road, tire tracks at their feet. Michael takes in the view, and inhales the crisp air, not a hint of garbage or smoke like he'd smell back home. Also unlike home, the silence weighing upon him is palpable. No people talking, running cars, screaming or shouting, ambulance and police sirens—utterly nothing but the wind and ice skittering across the frozen landscape. A discomfort settles over him, an uneasiness.

"And that's Hoven," Tabatha says, putting out her arms. "You like?"

"It's nice to be away from people, I can tell you that."

"Not all people, yes?"

He glances at her and smiles. "Not all, no."

She returns the gesture. "Want to go back? There is not much else besides what you have seen."

"Sure," he says, turning the way they came. "But if no one has electricity and the town's only this big, what does everyone do around here?"

"Let me show you."

Michael almost goes on a tangent about how he needs to be clearheaded for tonight, how he doesn't really drink, when Tabatha places a beer in front of him on the same table he sat at before. But he feels if he says anything, it very well could ruin what possible interest she may have in him. *It'll calm my nerves at least.* Tabatha occupies the seat next to him, takes a swig, and watches him do the same, the crisp, cold drink refreshing. Townsfolk occupy the tables around them more than any time prior, the room filled with chatter, laughter, cards being played, cigarette smoke drifting. Two couples sit by the fire, idly staring into the flames.

"You like?" she says over the din.

He nods, looking at the label as though he knows anything about beer. It's all in Norwegian. "Local?"

"Yes, brewed just a town over."

He's run out of things to talk about, his mind wandering.

Is this really the place they'll be? These people are...happy? I don't know why I expected them to be meaner. It doesn't make them not cultists, either. How many serial killers pass off as normal?

The evidence he does have—the trees with the star, the painted rocks over the mantel, the ominous "holiday," and the foot tracks going into the woods—seems flimsy at best, but there's too many coincidences for him to be wholly wrong. *Agnarr died here, and ITRUEND did say something happens here tomorrow.* Moreover, not everyone in Hoven is there in Hundehus. Those involved may be elsewhere in town, preparing for whatever.

Michael goes to take a swig, realizing he already finished it off. She leans over to him, hand on his shoulder, saying into his ear, "Want one more?"

His face is warm but he can't decide if it's from the alcohol. *No* sticks in his mouth, not wanting her to not be this close, her warm breath on his face. He yearns for her to be even closer, lips on him, his flesh tingling with an excitement he hasn't felt in ages. His heart races... But presuming what he wants her to be doing and what she actually is doing would become sour quickly if he's wrong.

"Sure," he says. "I'd like another." He can't keep his eyes from following her walking back into the kitchen with the empties. Rubbing his face, he forces himself to refocus no matter how hard it is.

This has to be the place, but where, though? The woods? Lots of cults do rituals in the woods, so maybe they're not any different. I'll just have to wake up at midnight and stay up the whole day. There'll be some sort of sign: people walking to the trees or cars starting or fires burning. They wouldn't bother being discreet if everyone's in on it.

Then he'll be face-to-face with the bastards, still without a plan. Somehow it feels liberating and terrifying all at once. Free from his self-induced cage when all he's known is the cage—he misses it, if he's honest with himself. Apprehension and anticipation swell. The urge to run out of the inn, out of Hoven, and take a plane back home overwhelms Michael. But... *They* killed *him, remember. They killed* hundreds *of innocent animals for a god that doesn't even fucking exist. Abandoning everything now is abandoning him.*

Tabatha comes back with six bottles, all of them clanging together on the table. "So I do not have to get up for more," she says, smiling. Her cheeks flush.

He's unsure if he's more glad she's back or for the relief more beer will bring.

A closing door wakes Michael. His eyelids are weighty when he opens them, saliva soaked into the pillow beneath his head. A sour tang coats his tongue. *Was that a dream or what?* He's sore all over, and sitting up, the dark room blurs. He blinks the grogginess away, rubbing his head and wiping his lips.

He shouldn't have had those beers, a lightweight; one became two, two to three, then four, but he's glad he did anyway. Grinning, he fondly goes through his memories of the last few hours before he and Tabatha fell asleep. He hasn't slept with anyone else besides Kayla. That feeling of infatuation teenagers are susceptible to—intoxicated by lust, by something new—embraces him. Not quite love, but something like. The honeymoon phase.

He puts his hand where she should be to find it empty, warm. "Tabatha?" Without an answer, he slides out of bed and checks the bathroom. She's not there, either. *Was I a one-night stand? Was she?* Michael scratches his head, going back to the bed, eyes landing on the alarm clock. 00:45 a.m. "Shit!"

Quickly he collects his clothes balled up by the wall and puts them on. From his luggage he puts on an extra pair of socks, and stares idly at the purple satchel among his things. His disbelief tempts him to leave it behind, but Olaf made it seem very important. If the Followers *do* do something...*supernatural*, he may want it on him just in case, so he pockets it.

Down the hall, none of the doors have the *No* plaque on their knobs, the inn strangely quiet. In the lobby, smoldering embers in the fireplace dimly bask the vacant tables in a weak glow. The chandeliers are unlit. He hears something rattling outside, metal clanging, maybe a chain or something. Wood creaks in the wind. As he cuts to the front door, a metallic noise coming from the back room stops him. *Is that where she went, to get a late-night snack?* Should he go see her, or leave her alone? Michael doesn't want to pull her into the mess he might soon be in, dragging her along into the unknown, but to not say at least goodbye doesn't sit right with him. Their hookup might've been only sex, but he'd still feel guilty leaving. *It'll just take a few minutes.*

Through the short hall, he enters the kitchen, illuminated by moonlight coming in from a large window by a closed back door in the rear.

Wooden counters run along the far walls, a heavily used butcher block in the middle of the room, a meat grinder bolted to it. Styrofoam coolers and other sorts of containers are stacked on the floor. A small oven, pots and pans on the stove burners, and cabinets are on the opposite side. Beyond stands an open metal freezer door, mist billowing. *Why would she need one of these, if no one stays year-round?*

Tabatha walks out wearing fitted black clothes from head to toe, her hair in a high bun, carrying—"*No*," Michael gasps, his stomach dropping. An image bursts in his mind: interlaced black lines going up a jaw, down a snout, back up between yellow eyes, passing pointed ears, meeting and forming the *Svulek* in the center. Green eyes in the cutout. *Her green eyes.*

She's ITRUEND? The guy in the video? How? Why? Am I still sleeping? Drunk? Did someone drug me last night?

Tabatha spins toward him, gazes meeting.

"That mask—why do you have that fucking mask?"

She glances at the wolf mask as though she isn't aware she's holding it. Looks up at him. "What about it?"

"You're one of them, the Followers," he says, disheartened. *And we had sex! With one of the Followers!* Stomach acid nips at the back of his throat, and he grabs the doorframe for support. His vision lags, a slowing heartbeat in his ears. "You killed Zylo."

"We would not do that," she says. "You told me it was a hit-and-run."

"I lied, it was you who did it—who—who *fucking* murdered my dog and stole his fucking organs!" His voice echoes in the silence.

"I am sorry, Michael, but we did not *murder* anyone. We *never* kill purposelessly. We harvest the offerings."

Surprisingly, he laughs. Her excuse is inane. "It doesn't matter what you want to call it or how you justify it to yourself. You. Killed. Him. Disemboweled him. Carved his fucking insides!"

"Your dog was meaningless then, but now he serves a greater purpose," she says plainly, "and soon your pain will be gone. Soon everyone's, everywhere, will be gone. Tonight we will heal the world."

"It was for nothing!" Anger overcomes misery. Rage compounds in his skull. Michael steps toward her, hands clenched. "There is no Fenrir.

There are no gods. You fucking idiots killed hundreds of animals for some dumbass pipe dream."

"I wish we had more time together—I could help you understand, see that what has been done was necessary. You could be with us, with *me*, but there is no more time left." Tabatha turns toward the back door. "We did not know each other long, but I will miss you, Michael."

"Don't you fucking go!" He runs after her. "You people can't get away with this."

Ignoring him, Tabatha slips into the night, and through the window Michael sees her run in the direction of the front of the inn. But when he catches a glimpse of the inside of the freezer—a small pile of frozen dogs on one side, underbellies flayed, entrails missing, eyes wide and unseeing; the other side full of metal shelving with wax paper on each, holding slabs and strips of meat—his legs immediately freeze. He doubles over, vomiting.

Did she—? The meat? No, no, no—I couldn't have. I couldn't. I would know. I could tell. I would. Should. Could. He groans before vomiting again. Michael wishes to take steel wool to his insides, to scrap every speck that shouldn't be there from him.

But he can't. The reality is he can't do anything for them, not now, except go after Tabatha. To do *something*. He can't let her get away. He can't let them all not be answered for. No longer solely for his own pup, but for every one of them around the world.

Michael doesn't look again. Once is too many. He staggers out the back door, keeping his legs from buckling, his gut from upheaving once more. The frigid air feels amazing on his sweaty skin. Footprints in the snow run pass a running generator and out around the inn to the front; he finds more going from the inn down the shoveled footpaths they walked the day before.

Cottages seem abandoned when he quickly peers through the windows: no cars out front; no lights, no fires, no candles lit; counters and tabletops bare. From their doors, more footprints heading in the same direction as the others. Michael reaches the outskirts, the trail leading into the forest beyond the frozen plain. *That's where they are.* Cars and trucks are parked off to the side, driverless. One of the truck beds smells of copper. Facing the woods, moonlight makes the landscape sparkle. Vague orangish lights flicker like torches within the trees, gradually shrinking. Ice skitters as a breeze blows, stinging his nose.

Before he lets himself rest, to think, to be afraid, he trudges through onward. Soon, spruces loom over him, undersides black against the pale light, the forest floor engulfed in broken shadows. Boles feel like they're closing in around him, less space to walk, and at the same time it seems that there are fewer than before.

Ahead, the bobbing lights stay in view. *How haven't I got any closer?* His throat and lungs are on fire, and he lost feeling in his toes a while ago. His gloves and pockets do little to keep his hands warm. Still, he moves as fast as his body allows while being cautious, not wanting to slip on gnarled roots or trip and bash his head on a trunk.

Soon, the *Svulek* appears in the dark brown bark, branded. He's tempted to touch one, but what good would it do when his fingers are numb? Breathing labored, he pushes on, far slower than he was when he started. The dancing light abruptly vanishes and dread floors him. *Am I going to get lost?* Moonlight can be seen above, but a cloud could block it any moment.

He pauses mid-stride, holding his breath, waiting for something, anything… A massive fire blooms in the distance, firelight trickling through the woods. Dull droning unfurls in the atmosphere, a throaty hum like someone doing it right in his ears. *What is that? Sounds like something I'd hear in church.* Although he yearns to quicken towards the light, he follows it slowly. Snow's flattened by so many prints. Droning becomes louder, seamlessly changing into a melody so high-pitched he can't discern if words are being spoken or not. The hair on the back of his neck stands, something akin to static electricity charging the air.

Michael smells fresh-cut wood before he discovers trees giving way to stumps, ground blanketed in wood dust, spruce needles, and skeletal branches. Now he can make out the tip of a bonfire in the distance. It grows the closer he comes. The Followers are black figures against the flames that seemingly reach the low, gibbous moon, orange bleeding into it. *What the hell is that? Doesn't matter.* Fatigue melts away, adrenaline giving him a second wind. He clenches his jaw, striding forward. *Who cares if they hear me now? Fuck them.*

As he enters the humanmade clearing, he hears a noise behind him, but before he can react, someone snatches his arm, the other. The backs of his knees are kicked and he drops to the earth. Michael glances at the two robed people gripping his arms, faces partially hidden by sheer black.

"Let me go!" He tries to pull himself free but fails. "You mother—"

The Followers part and Tabatha slips out, walking toward them. The lines running over the wolf mask glean, somehow. She stops, lifting the mask and crouching. "It is fate that you are here, Michael. You could have left, could have gone anywhere, but you came *here*."

"Where else would I go, you lunatic? We're in the middle of fucking nowhere!"

Her black-leather-gloved fingers raise his face by his chin. "We are at the most important place in this world."

He violently shakes her hand from him. "I'm not going to let you get away with this. You're dog killers," he screams, spittle flying. "You're fucking scum—you deserve to be gutted like they were, your fucking bodies thrown onto that fire. *You'd serve a purpose then.*"

"We harvested what's necessary." She repeats, unfazed, her peridot eyes widening. "This world has been meaningless for a long time—*we* will give it meaning tonight. We will bring the dawn of a new age, Michael, one that we have wanted for centuries."

She straightens, putting the mask back on.

"What do you want us to do with him?" one of the Followers says.

"He can witness the divine, but only that."

Nothing in response, and Tabatha walks back to the bonfire.

"Come back here!" Michael attempts to get his legs under him, thrashing. "Come back here, you bitch!" Sobs come, choking him. "You—you took him... You took him and I will—I will..." *Do nothing.*

She passes through her congregation as though they're a curtain, their throaty melody uninterrupted.

Tears fall to the ground, his newfound strength leaving him, *I can't do this. I can't confront her or any of them. Why did I think this would work? How could I be such an idiot? I should've listened to Kayla, let the police handle it, and stayed home with Aaron to be sure not to miss X-Mas. No, I might not see either of them again... I wish I could just be a normal fucking person sometimes, or ever.*

A word he doesn't understand is shouted and they immediately fall silent, causing him to look up. Unsettling quiet lingers among the clearing. In unison, the Followers take a step back, and Michael discovers they weren't standing around the fire, but a pit dug before the fire. With her back to him, Michael can tell Tabatha hasn't moved; flames dance over her silhouette, casting a long shadow across the white.

Then she treads around the hole. One by one, others follow her until they return to the rim. They pause and crouch, brushing away white. They remove silver-hilted daggers from beneath their robes, Tabatha's gilded, and plunge them into the damp earth. Carving, seemingly writing something Michael can't discern, but he assumes it's the *Svulek. What else could it be?*

Weapons are tugged out, placed at their feet, and they rise together. Tabatha yells in an unknown language, and the rest do the same until their voices overlap into an incoherent cacophony. Above, the moon expands—or *nears*. The bonfire erupts as though doused in gasoline, flames ascending, splintering and cupping the moon's bottom. What pale light it casts darkens; vermilion droplets trickle skyward into the moon, rippling as though a serene pond. It fills, casting everything into a blood-orange hue.

Michael watches wide-eyed, mouth agape, loss and anger—everything leading up to now—temporarily forgotten, the entirety of his plight no more a memory than the last time he took his pills.

"What the hell is going on?" he mutters, fear coiling around his chest, pushing air from his lungs. A sharp wind burns his watering eyes, but he *can't* look away, wouldn't move even if he could. Not only had he been wrong to pursue the cult, but he has been fucking wrong about all of it. Gods or not, something unreal, *inhuman*, occurs right in front of him. If his mind wasn't frayed and depleted, he couldn't possibly explain what he's witnessing.

Something boils, groaning. Something the same color of the moon bubbles from where they had carved in the ground. Gentle illuminance flickers over them from below, revealing glimpses of some of them smiling, others crying, a few enraptured. The viscous substance spills over the lip and into the pit.

Michael's jaw drops.

The group banshee screams. More fluid oozes into the hole. More boiling. More hissing. Sharp pain stabs the back of Michael's eyes, his head immediately throbbing. Trees shake around them, clattering, powder and needles falling, ice breaking throughout the forest.

Something rises from the pit. *The organs.*

Endless layers of steaming, churned innards swell like an expanding bubble, red-orange treacle bleeding from runes etched into the organs. A deep breath throws back some of the Followers' hoods. Michael registers their appearances quickly: just about every hair color and cut, every skin tone he can name; some covered in sweat and breathing hard; protruding brows and chins, large noses and thin lips, bulging and deep-seated eyes. Weirdly, he's glad there's diversity, coming together to end the world.

The organs tower over all. The vermilion liquid blackens, solidifying. Melding everything into one layer, a grotesque quilt. A segment tears, black sludge spilling, another, then another, tar sluicing out in rivulets. Rot and filth overtake any pleasant aromas the forest can offer. A grating growl booms from miles away yet near enough it devours the group's call.

Steel thunders against steel. The growl multiplies, numberless packs of wild dogs hunting down their prey. Jaws snap and gnash. Iron squeals, being torn asunder. An earthquake radiates underfoot, shaking Michael's insides. *This isn't an earthquake.* He realizes. *Whatever's coming is getting stronger, louder,* closer. Soon the cultists who hold him have trouble standing like the rest of them as each resounding reverberation—

Gore explodes, blowing the cult off their feet, slamming onto the ground.

"Holy shit," Michael says.

A colossal snout lances from the hole, a snarling, frothing mouth and ivory fangs the size of stalagmites. Glistening oil covers its matted fur. Bright, piercing vermilion eyes under a jutting, furrowed brow quickly takes in its surroundings. Fissures bolt through the earth as who must be Fenrir emerges from the pit, leaping into the sky. An enormous tattered, gloved hand careens to the earth, halted by the fallen trees.

Followers scream, some scrambling to their feet, reeling back. Others remain lying, frozen by terror. Among the frenzy, Tabatha kneels with open arms toward the sky.

"Fuck this," a cultist holding him says, releasing him, darting into the woods.

The other mutters something, then he's gone, too.

Michael has the urge to stop them and force them to face Fenrir, scream in their faces: "You did this! This is what you fucking wanted!"

The Devourer of Worlds lands in front of the bonfire, towering over the high flames, the forest. Titanic. A four-legged, canine god. Even from where he is, Michael cranes his neck back to see him fully. Fur ripples like gasoline on water. Slivers open and close between the folds of his draping flesh, like thousands of tiny mouths gasping for air. Ichor seeps down bared fangs, melting snow, burning grass. An ancient, cracked sword through his jaws shatters, disintegrating; its rusted hilt disappears down his gullet.

Michael's aware he should be like the congregation escaping into the woods, but he keeps himself from running. He might've been unable to do anything to avenge his pup, but he *can* at least witness the demise of the bastards who took him. Their deaths will justify sacrificing time with his son, time he'll never get back. It will bring justice to every other dog owner in the world, if they know it or not.

Everything happens too fast and too slow simultaneously. Two Followers trip over tree stumps, tumbling. A handful slip in the slush, catching others by their robes, bringing them down with them. In one fluid motion, Fenrir kicks up wet earth, bounding across the clearing, taking worshippers into his open maw. The utter mayhem thereafter is too quick to discern.

Bones snap, break, crunch, joining the frantic symphony. Meat's eviscerated. Sinew and viscera stream from his mouth. Bowels spurt from carnal cavities fallen to the wayside. Treacle splashes treetops, singes on flames, and stains snow scarlet. They are devoured thoughtlessly, insignificant as ants, faith and servitude hollow. A few make it to the safety of the spruces, but Michael's sure they won't make it far.

Copper, rot, and shit burn Michael's sinuses, cloys the back of his throat. Fenrir laps at his spoils, as though the meal of dozens hasn't touched his eons-long hunger. Insatiable. Unrelenting. Sublime.

"Devourer of Worlds!" Tabatha screams, nearing the god, her arms still raised. Her mask had fallen at some point, wiry blonde hair free from a ponytail, speckled by blood. Her smile's ear to ear, wide eyes misty.

She's happy about this. Ecstatic. What a lunatic.

"We welcome you to our world! We're joyous that your journey and our work was successful." She stops before his flank, him working on the gore. "We have given you ample offerings, we plead to you to begin Ragnarok, like you were destined to. We beg of you to push the world to extinction, to bring about the new era with us by your side, your dedicated Followers."

Fenrir digs his nose deeper into the dirt, attempting to consume every last morsel. Michael almost laughs at the scene, reminding him of when he walked away for two seconds from his food to come back to find Zylo eating from his plate. He wouldn't stop no matter how many times he shouted at him to. At least *someone* ate dinner that night.

Tabatha's brow pinches. "Fenrir! We have offered more than enough to you. We *brought* you here—you *must* obey us, or—or we'll send you back!"

Can she even do that?

Fenrir lifts his head, looking at her behind him. His breath blows her hair back.

As Tabatha begins a diatribe, Michael realizes two things: Once she's been eaten, there will be no one else left to eat besides him; and if *he's* gone, Fenrir will continue forever, that the world *will* be devoured.

Shit. I have to stop him somehow.

Michael takes in the clearing, sight landing on the giant hand lying nearby. Tattered cloth's strewn around its coarse, heavily scarred fingers; a rusted silver bracer engraved in runes covers its hairy forearm; taut, puckered flesh covers where it was severed from the elbow.

What was this called? I definitely read something about this on the Internet. I know it's important, that it does something. It's a part of a god, but what the hell is anyone supposed to do with it?

He side-eyes Tabatha and Fenrir, the latter now turned around, head low toward her. She continues rambling on about what they did for him, what they will do, and so forth. Michael slowly stands and walks toward the hand, stepping lightly over the carnage at his feet, a sea of bodies and blood. The hand goes up to his shoulders, each finger the size of his torso. Chiseled into its palm is an etching of a flat mountain beneath a circle.

Michael scans the clearing, as if an answer to his dilemma can be found there, seeking guidance from a slaughterhouse. He longs for someone—anyone—to tell him what the fuck to do. Thoughts ricochet in his skull, once more drawing from the question: *What would I do if this was a story?* It worked before, and it's all he has to use.

If it was a book, there'd be a connection... A connection between the hand and...the fire. Yeah, the fire would be important because... No, not the fire, the pit. It's important because it's...it's a well? No, dumb. Important because...it's...where he came from, so it would be the way for him to leave through. And the arm, the arm would follow the same logic. It held Fenrir when he came out, so maybe it needs to be in there to pull him back?

Nothing else comes to him, so he decides on that plan. Before shoving the hand, Michael rechecks the pair. Tabatha has stopped talking, is standing closer to him, one arm held out as if she's going to pet him. Fenrir's vermilion eyes watch her, teeth surprisingly not bared. *Why hasn't he left? There's so much more to eat out there.* Either way, he's running out of time, no matter what happens.

The hand rolls easily but is extremely dense, like pushing a boulder. Michael digs his feet into the ground, veins rising in his neck, cursing. His shoulders and quads are ablaze. His lower back wails. Breathing out his mouth does little to calm his heart. *I need to exercise more after all this.* He peeks over the arm to find the pit a couple feet away. Tabatha's hand rests on Fenrir's head. She's speaking fast, too low to make out.

He makes it to the pit, now a vat of dark sludge, reeking of gelatin, weirdly. Still unsure if he's right or not, he shoves it in. It rolls into the goop, squelching. While it sinks, fruity decay wafts out. Quicker than anticipated, it's submerged, gone...

Nothing happens. *Fuck. Don't panic. It might take a minute to work. Patience.* Maybe a minute goes by and nothing happens, again. In frustration, he kicks the rust-colored dirt in, praying that's the key... Nada. Sweating, he quickly looks back to them.

Fenrir's head is raised, glaring at him. Gore smears his snout, flesh dangling from his bottom jaw like clothes on a line. He shows his fangs, plastered with humanity. Eyes aglow. Tabatha stands beside his leg, pointing at Michael.

"Oh no." Back to the pit, he screams: "Work! For the love of God, fucking do something!"

I had to have read something about this somewhere.

His terrified eyes rove the ground as if words are written there. Websites. Books. Articles. All a flurry of bullshit, a blankness fucked by fear.

I can't remember!

His lungs flutter and his insides are carved empty and he wants to sob and pout and shout and run and *Jesus Christ, I'm going to die—*

The satchel in his coat moves.

What the hell?

He takes it out and something kneads the bag from the *inside*. Opening it, the scent of birds barely registers. Gray cat paws move, furry toes wiggling; the pink curved things inflate and deflate, *breathing*; roots and hair grow, slithering around the rapidly pulsating red-and-purple fibers in sync with Michael's heartbeat.

The ground shakes and Fenrir's in the sky. Without a second thought he repeats what he did with the arm, dumping the ribbon into the goop. Then he hunkers and wraps his arms around his head, preparing for the unpreparable. He thinks of Aaron, of Zylo, of Kayla, of his house in Carlysle City, of the books he had written and those he hasn't, of his life. Past, present, and future. Remembrances overlap, flashing behind his closed eyelids like fast-forwarded home movies. Screams boom in his head. Michael doesn't want to die, not only because of all he's done, accomplished, seen, but what he hasn't done, *could* do, will do, or fix given the opportunity by fate, gods—whoever or whatever's watching him pray more than he ever has before. He'll do anything to see tomorrow.

I love you, Aaron.

I love you, Zylo.

I love you, Kayla.

I'm sorry. I'm sorry, so sorry.

A gale flings what feels like hot oil on him, throwing him back. The sticky substance sears his flesh, burns through his coat and clothes, but the fight-or-flight mode keeps the pain in the foreground. Opening his eyes, he shouts, frantically peeling off the black ichor like dry wax. Hair and skin tear off with it, leaving dark oblong scars covering his body, holes throughout his clothes.

A brilliance explodes from a crude opening in the black pit. The moon hangs low, no longer orange but pearl. The sky's aquamarine, the stars chartreuse. The giant hand—now mountainous—has risen from the opening, the *Svulek* in its palm frothing with magnificent colors, golden dew trickling down its vascular forearm. Fenrir's throat in its grasp. The Devourer of Worlds futilely attempts to free himself by kicking with his hind legs, but can't pierce the bracer. Yelping, he tries his front legs to escape, and when that fails, he gnashes at the coiled fingers, but he can't move his head enough to find purchase.

Roots sprout, ascending like unfurling ivy up the arm, through the dew and curling between fingers. Crescent-shaped bright pink glands inflate along branching ends, hanging heavy like bell flowers from spiraling strands. Cat paws trot and prance over and under Fenrir's throat, bells chiming each delicate step, red-and-purple threads and braided hair twined around their ankles, forming a noose around Fenrir's gullet. They jerk taut and Fenrir whimpers, a black tear swirled through with misty vermillion falling from the end of his eye. His tongue hangs out his panting mouth.

Briefly, guilt washes over Michael. *It's not his fault. They summoned him. He didn't ask to be here. He didn't ask for what happened to him in the other world, chained to a rock with a sword keeping his mouth shut forever. What would anyone else expect from an abused dog? The blame isn't his. It's the owners.* But Michael's aware that keeping Fenrir free would be obviously bad, no matter who caused what.

The hand plummets into the ichor, taking Fenrir with it. The opening collapses unto itself, radiance dissipating like gilded dust motes. Treacle bubbles once, then settles, cooling. No indication of what it had been or what came out of it. Black returns to the sky, white to the stars, and pale light to the moon. A soft blue appears on the horizon. The bonfire, mostly forgotten, dwindles to smoldering kindling. As suddenly as the world was at the brink of destruction, it was no more.

Michael props himself up on his elbows. His breath is fog, the chill of winter reemerging. It doesn't calm his nerves, his body teeming with seemingly every emotion possible. Silence hangs over the clearing. He stares at the hole. *Is it over—*

Screaming, Tabatha tackles him. They roll through bloody mud and slush. When they come to a stop, Tabatha's atop him, left hand raised overhead wielding a dagger. He holds her arm back while the other fights with her right hand pressing on his neck. Michael didn't expect her to be so strong. Blood stains her scarred, pale face, burned into the wrinkles of her brow. Her teeth clenched, seething. Air struggles to get into his lungs. He feels lightheaded. Vision vignetting. His hand holding back the knife weakens, weakens...

It drops, but he manages to roll away before the blade plunges into him, stabbing into the earth. He uses his weight to carry Tabatha with him, unbalancing her. She drops onto her side, and despite his throat wheezing to replenish the air he had lost, he crawls on top of her.

His knees keep her arms pinned, her hand flailing in an attempt to grab the fallen knife, the rest of his body leaned over her upper torso, forehead pressing against hers. She smells horrible. Tabatha tries to bite him like the god before her but he raises his head up enough to avoid it. Strength and sight come back to him, and he straightens.

"You ruined it!" she spits. "You filth, you horrible little man. We were at the gates of Valhalla and you closed them!"

Michael takes the dagger for reasons beyond him, holding it over her.

"Kill me, Michael! I have no more purpose now he's gone. Do me this last favor, please. I do not want to see this world anymore."

He stares at the serrated weapon, crimson-stained. *What the hell am I doing? I'm not a killer.* And even if he wanted to, he wouldn't. Truly, Michael doesn't give a shit about her anymore, about any of it. He's found who killed Zylo and watched them get their just desserts. Murdering Tabatha won't make him feel any more satisfied than he is now. Though he'd be lying to himself if he doesn't believe punching her in the face wouldn't feel *really* good, but he's never been one for violence.

Alone, she's useless. The Followers might try again sometime in the future, and he may very well get involved then, but for now it's done. Over. He has more important things waiting for him back home. She continues on her tangent, begging for him to end her. *The knife is cool, though, but I can't take it on the plane...* He throws it as far as he can, and gets to his feet.

Tabatha doesn't move, staring up at him. "You are not going to hurt me for what we did?"

"No," he says, putting his hands in his jacket pockets. "Enough's been done already."

Michael has a gut feeling he's facing the right way back to Hoven, but also the Followers' footprints should lead him there, so he starts that way. As he steps around the mangled mess of meat, bone, and black cloth left behind, he kicks a polished black stone, stark against the white. He picks it up and brushes it off to find it filled with cloudy red-orange. *Fenrir's tear? It must've fell when he was dragged under.* Michael considers tossing it back, finished with all this esoteric bullshit, but he rather have it than Tabatha. Taking it, he heads onward, soon passing the tree line.

"Do not leave me!" she shouts, echoing. "You bastard! Come back, Michael!"

He can't help smirking, irony not lost to him.

The sun makes the black robes thrown on the ground contrast harshly on the white field. When the wind blows, Michael's scars burn fiercely. *Well, if they're not using them.* He grabs one of them on his way across. What parked vehicles there were are gone, ruts in the street, slushy square-shaped bare patches. All the quilts, books, anything resembling the homes' occupants are gone. The fire mantels and trees are bare. Only dust and ash left. He wonders if they would've done the same if their plan didn't turn out the way it did. *Probably not.*

The flurry of feet continues to the inn, and inside everything's a mess. Tables and chairs upturned, fireplace barren, chandeliers extinguished; behind the counter is ransacked, shelves and key rack in disarray. He avoids the kitchen. Down the hall, all the doors to the rooms beside his stand open, as abandoned as the cottages. He's a little surprised they didn't burn the village down, if they were concerned about their connection to the bloodbath. His room key is still in his pants, sticky with congealed blood; he cleans it on the robe before unlocking the door.

He grabs the pill bottle left on the nightstand, pops the cap, and gulps one down. Afterward, he takes a shower, realizing the generator isn't on when the warm water runs out. Taken aback by his reflection, he stares into the deep-seated, bleary eyes of a person who looks nothing like himself from before Zylo's passing. Gray strips like impressions of thick leeches scar his pale skin. They run up his neck, lay across his hollow cheeks and forehead; parts of his eyebrows have burned off. Sunken, coarse, and ridged to the touch. Leaning into the mirror, he discovers they're not ridged with lines but tiny rows of runes, nearly microscopic. Michael strains his vision to read them—

He reels back, runs his hands over his face. "Not dealing with this now."

He leaves the bathroom, gets dressed in clean clothes, and packs. His wallet's still in the back pocket of his old pants, thankfully, which he leaves behind with the other destroyed clothes and the hijacked cultist robe. *Someone else can deal with that.*

Outside, he strides in the ruts on the road toward the bus stop outside of town. Countryside overtakes the village, forest pushed back to the horizon. *Where did they all go? There were a lot when we got there. I guess most of them are dead, so maybe there weren't many left? Were there that many cars?* He can't remember. About a mile from Hoven, he reaches the bus stop. He brushes fresh snow from the metal bench and sits. He puts his luggage between his feet, and holds his face in his hands and takes the extra time he may have to sleep.

Sometime later, the arriving bus wakes him. Grabbing his stuff, he gets onto it once it stops. It takes a beat to find money to pay the fee, and the bus driver, wearing a Santa hat, eyes him when the silver coins are stained red, but he takes them anyway. "Jingle Bells" issues from the speakers. At the back of the vehicle, Michael watches Hoven gradually recede.

I never want to see this fucking place ever again.

After spending an obscene amount of money he doesn't have on a plane ticket and bus fare to get back to Carlysle City, his home, Michael doesn't bother going inside. He chucks his belongings onto his snow-covered porch, shakes off his bike leaning against the side, and forces his dead legs to pedal to Kayla's. Arriving, he nearly falls with the bike when he tries to get off it in her shoveled walkway. He trudges up the salted stairs two at a time, and knocks on the door.

Kayla opens it.

"*Michael*, what happened to you?" Her wide brown eyes take him in.

"I'll explain later," he says. "Can I see Aa—"

"Dad!" Aaron shouts, running around Kayla, and wraps his arms around Michael's waist. He picks him up beneath his arms, and embraces him. Tears flow as he recalls Fenrir leaping toward him, the utter dread, his frantic heart in his throat, the screaming in his skull—the last seconds of life he believed he had left. His arms tighten around his son.

"Oh, buddy," he says. "I missed you so much."

"Me too, Dad." He stares into Michael's eyes, gingerly touching the scar on his cheek, a prickle of pain shooting through Michael's face. "Does it hurt?"

He laughs, shaking his head. "Not at all, bud."

"Did you see the police about Zylo? Is he still doing good?"

"Yup, and he's doing very good." *One day I'll tell him.* "Did you finish your list for Santa?"

Focus shifted, Aaron says: "Yeah! Wanna see it?"

Michael glances at Kayla. "If it's fine with your mom."

She nods. "Of course, come in." As he does, she says: "You hungry?"

The meat on his plate blurs through his mind, vomiting in the kitchen; what he found in the freezer. His mouth fills with saliva, acid in his empty stomach threatening to come up. He pushes the horrors away, the nausea down.

"Starving."

Michael stays until Aaron falls asleep on the floor, his list and colored marker in his hands. Kayla offers to drive him home, but he insists he'd rather ride his bike instead. The silent, gabled houses covered in snow with Christmas lights lining their roofs and windows are soothing; the cloudless, evening sky calming; the sound of his tires on the slushy pavement relaxing in some odd way. His belongings haven't moved from his porch. He unlocks the front door, and removes the mail stuffed into his mailbox and carries it inside.

Standing in the entry, the emptiness of his home presses upon him. It's been however long but he briefly still expects Zylo to gallop downstairs, hear his nails clacking on the wood, and leap on him... Grabbing Fenrir's tear from his bag he sets aside, putting the mail on top, he goes into the kitchen, and retrieves the box containing his dog's ashes from the top cabinet. He rubs his thumb over it.

"Miss you, boy. More than ever."

After placing him and the tear on the counter, Michael takes them in for a moment. On the plane he thought maybe it would bring some semblance of peace having the start and finish of the whole journey, but the black stone reminds him more of what he lost and to what. It makes him want to throw it out the fucking window.

I'll deal with it later.

Going upstairs, he isn't sure what to do or where to go now. His life until now solely consisted of avenging him, and the future is simply unknowable. But the one thing he does know is this: He doesn't want to forget anything, the good or bad. He refuses for the memory of Zylo to fade like the countless lives of parents, grandparents, loved ones, strangers, people on the news. Their lives and deaths a blip on the radar for a few hours, at best, then they wither away, only recollected sparingly like antiques in an attic.

He's more than that.

He opens his closed bedroom door. Blankets nestled on the mattress, his pet's bed, half-full water dish, his toy lying on the carpet. Same as it was that awful night. Michael's still not ready, but peering into the room, it doesn't hurt as much. *Wonder how it'll feel to sleep in there, again...* "Probably will have to buy a new bed."

He walks into his office and notices a book he bought from Olaf on the desk. *Must've forgot it while packing.* Michael had forgotten about him practically since leaving for Olso, but now he recalls him wanting a souvenir in exchange for the ribbon. *He never told me what to do if it's gone. Also never gave me his address, either.* Michael doesn't think he'd be able to find his shop again even if he scoured the city. Fenrir's tear pops in his head. *That should work for a souvenir. Just have to wait for him to contact me or show up.*

Moving the book and switching on the computer, he sits in front of it, opening a word document. The thing, he believes, that stands the test of time, keeping people alive throughout generations, are books, music, movies, photographs. He's not a photographer, a musician, nor a film-maker. But he was—*is* a writer. And every reader and author knows stories hold power. A century can pass, but the same book can have the same profound effect, memories fresh and lively as they were initially.

He centers the cursor, sets his fingers onto the keys. It feels uncomfortable, weird, to return to what he lost, but life changes and he can either adapt or become lost, too.

Sighing, Michael types: *The Companions We Lose.*

ABOUT THE AUTHOR

Micah Castle writes weird fiction and horror. His stories have appeared in various magazines, websites, and anthologies. He's the author of *The Companions We Lose, Homecoming, The Women Without Eyes,* and *The World He Once Knew.*

While away from the keyboard, he enjoys spending time with his wife, playing with his animals, being in the woods, and can typically be found writing or reading a book somewhere in his Pennsylvania home.

You can find him at: www.micahcastle.com, www.patreon.com/micahcastle, or on other platforms: www.linktr.ee/micahcastle.

THE REAL ZYLO

Zylo X-mas '98

Zylo was my first "real" pet, growing up with me from about seven-years-old until he passed when I was around nineteen-years-old.

He was a Chihuahua Rat Terrier mix and like owners of either of those breeds knows, he never seemed to lose energy, always wanted to play, and barked *a lot*. Nevertheless, he was a very good boy.

We gave him the best life he could have and even though it's been fifteen or so years since he's been here, I find myself still missing him.

IF YOU ENJOYED THIS BOOK...

Please consider rating or reviewing wherever books are sold. They go a long way to helping the book find more great readers like you.

If you want to support another way, consider signing up to my newsletter: www.micahcastle.com/newsletter. You'll receive a free ebook for doing so.

Content Warnings

Animal Violence, Animal Death, Animal Abuse, Violence, Murder